Healing His Heart

Annie Seaton

Sunshine Coast: Book 3

ANNIE SEATON

Chapter One

Liam Wyndham rested the paddle on the front of the kayak while he caught his breath. The small waves at the beach break rocked the small craft gently in the light breeze. He'd been paddling for an hour and had managed to clear his mind—almost. He looked up to the top of the cliff and examined the sprawling old house that looked to be teetering on the edge of the rocky cliff.

The view of the house was completely different from the sea. Located ten kilometres south of Noosa, it suited him very well. There was only one other house close by and it had been in darkness, with no sign of life in the week since he'd moved in.

Apparently, according to the local real estate agent, the owners had moved interstate for work, and that made the location even more attractive. He wanted no interruptions and desired no neighbourly company. All he wanted was a place where he could lick his wounds and think about his future. With online communication and a huge stash of groceries, he'd be able to bury himself with little disruption and get his damned book to his publisher. The only issue would be the workmen who were coming to build bookshelves for him, but once he let them in and showed them where to go, he'd stay out of their way.

Liam needed to find himself and his place in life after the hellish six months he'd just endured. If he was honest, he'd admit he needed more than a place to finish *Guardian of the Village,* his latest adventure book set in Nepal. He also needed space and solitude to regain some stability in his life after the shock of Vanessa's death. He'd been researching his book in the Himalayas and the media had had a field day, portraying him as the jet-setting author who always left his wife behind when he travelled. Vanessa had come up with that story for a trashy gossip magazine interview and it had spread like wildfire. Truth be known, she was the one who hadn't wanted to go with him.

"Why the hell would I want to go with you to a third world country?" She had stared at him, her heavily made-up eyes open wide. "No restaurants, no shops, and we've just been invited to three premieres—and the after-parties!"

Then, right before he'd left, she'd told him she was seeing someone else and was going to move out while he was in Nepal. So he'd gone off alone to research his latest book and hadn't cared one bit about missing the Sydney social scene. While in the Himalayas, he'd realised that he didn't miss Vanessa and being dragged around to the parties that his fame had given them entry to. He'd worked hard to make the money to keep her happy, but it hadn't been enough for her, so he had decided that he'd be happier alone, so he'd give her a divorce—and a settlement, whatever it took.

The pileup on the motorway that had resulted in Vanessa's death had left him numb, and a little guilty. Maybe if he'd tried harder to understand her, she would have stayed with him and not been out on that fateful night.

Then the vultures had come in for the kill, blaming him for leaving her alone. Liam had gotten sick of seeing his face plastered on all the entertainment sites and blogs. Sarah, his agent, had advised him to sue, but he had hoped the whole set of lies would die a natural death and they'd move on to their next victim. All Liam wanted was shut himself away from the world and write. It was all he'd ever wanted to do, and he wasn't going to get caught again. He intended to become a recluse. Uncle Joe had done just that in this house, and he would do it, too. Liam had never been comfortable in the false world of Sydney; attending celebrity events, the fancy restaurants and book signings had been at Vanessa's request. His wife had thrived on the publicity, until she'd found a more famous celebrity to hang on to. Ironic, really—she'd accused him of being unfaithful almost every time he'd signed a book for a female reader. Vanessa had been needy, and he hadn't been able to give her what she wanted.

It was too hard. Liam knew he didn't have it in him to pander to the demands of a clingy woman. Most of the time he was lost in his own thoughts and planning a scene, or setting up a plot, and he missed the cues that other guys just seemed to pick up on.

So he was here to bunker down and write. He didn't need people in his life. He had his books and enough travel memories and stories in his head to keep him writing for years. His days of travelling the world were over. He had a home, and he wasn't going anywhere.

For the life of him, he couldn't understand the macabre interest in his being widowed and what it had to do with entertaining the masses. The sales of his books had skyrocketed after the articles were published, but he didn't care. What he needed now was some privacy and peace. Then maybe the muse who had deserted him would return. He had been given three months to find it, or his deal with a top New York publisher was toast. No matter how well his previous books had sold, if he didn't deliver this book by Christmas, they were going to terminate the contract. He had four weeks left to write it. Even as he thought about it, dread rose into his throat and his mind went blank.

The wind picked up and the chill of late autumn settled on his bare shoulders as he lifted the paddle and headed for the shore. There was a trail at the base of the cliff leading up to the house. When he'd set out, the waves breaking on the beach had been tiny, but now he had to focus on paddling through the small swells that lapped at the kayak. He glanced behind him as a strong gust of wind pushed him closer to the shore and the kayak slewed around side-on to the waves. Liam knew he was going over and braced himself for the shock of the cold water.

***

"It's not you, it's me."

What a cop-out. The words ran like a mantra through Georgie Sacchi's head as she followed the trail to the beach. What was it about guys? Did they all gather around the bar together and come up with stock phrases to end a relationship with? Did they really believe any woman in her right mind would fall for it?

"Mutt, I swear, if you pull on your lead one more time, I'll…I'll…" A litany of swear words hovered on Georgie's lips and she grinned. She was known as one of the kindest, most even-tempered products of Maleny where she had grown up, and her friends would be horrified to hear a swear word cross her lips. They'd be even more surprised to read her dark thoughts this bleak afternoon.

Everyone saw her as a good sport. Happy, easy-going Georgie. Practical joker Georgie. Life-and-soul-of-the-party Georgie.

She'd toughened up in the weeks since her mother, Marietta, had died, only a couple of weeks after spilling the truth to Georgie and her "sister", Sienna that their lives had been a sham. For twenty-nine years, she and Sienna had believed they were fraternal twins. Not only had her mother told them they were actually cousins born on the same day, but she had also told them her cancer was terminal. Georgie had spent most of her mother's last days by her bedside, but they had never spoken of the deception again.

Sienna was her best friend in the whole world and Georgie's sounding board when things went wrong. Georgie didn't think it mattered if they were sisters or cousins. But Georgie had not told Sienna about the spectacular breakup with her latest man. "It's not you, it's me." When Brent had used the same line as Cole, and Harrison before him, Georgie had foolishly pressed him for details and his words had turned around to cut her.

"Not marriage material," he'd said. "You, not me."

In the weeks since then, Georgie had put on a brave face and carried on in her usual happy way. In front of her friends, anyway. The friends who were the problem, according to Brent.

"You hang around with old people." The look on his face had been full of disdain. In that moment, she had been happy to let him go.

Georgie's best friends—her age—were no longer around. Sienna was happy in her new life with Jack, living down in Noosa, and Ana had moved to Melbourne with her partner, Blake, and their baby, Faith.

Okay, so I'm happy for Sienna and Ana. They were in love but deep down Georgie carried a belief that she would never admit to her friends. Not in a million years: she was never going to find a partner and it was time to accept that.

Especially after Brent…and Cole…and Harrison…and—

Oh, shite. She wasn't going to waste any more time thinking about them. So she picked losers. Either that, or Brent's reason for breaking up with her was true. She just wasn't marriage or permanent relationship material. Maybe she did take after her mother.

It didn't matter anyway. Once she finished this rush job for Blake's hardware store, Georgie was heading out. She was going overseas and staying away from men…for good. Before Blake and Ana had left for Melbourne, Blake, her boss, had begged her to do this one small building job before she left on her big adventure. All of the other local builders were too busy, and the client wanted the work done immediately. It was convenient for her because the house was next door to the cottage where she was house-sitting until she left on her trip. She had agreed to delay her trip by a month to get it finished. She could put in long days. Georgie had pretended it was a big deal to change her ticket, but in reality, it had given her time to delay the trip. Yet now that Ana and Blake were in Melbourne and Sienna was at Noosa, she could drop the brave front she'd put up.

Georgie wasn't even sure she wanted to go away on this trip. It was going to take a lot of courage to leave behind all that was familiar, and a place she'd lived for twenty-nine years. A place where she'd been settled and content until Brent's final comment had made her take a long hard look at her life. But the trip was booked now, and her departure day was set in stone. Georgie was leaving from Brisbane on Christmas Eve. First stop, Honolulu. She had agreed to help out an old school friend and her husband and look after their animals over Christmas while they visited family, and she was living in their cottage in Hideaway Bay, down the coast from her hometown of Maleny. After that, she had an open round-the-world ticket…and the world was hers to discover.

Mutt leaped ahead as something moved on the trail in front of them and the leash pulled from her fingers. He disappeared over the sand dune onto the beach and Georgie hurried after him. By the time she'd reached the base of the dune and clambered over the piles of driftwood, he was in the water and was barking and jumping about in the shallows.

The sun was almost to the horizon in the west and Georgie put her hand up to her eyes to shield the silver glare reflecting on the water. She squinted as she spotted a small kayak floating upside down in the break. Mutt barked and took off toward a large log lying on the wet sand.

"Oh God." It wasn't a log, it was a person lying face down on the sand, and Georgie took off at a run. "Not a body, oh please, not a body."

The sun broke through the low cloud and bathed the beach in front of her in late-afternoon sunshine. As she ran toward the unmoving shape on the now-glistening sand, she dug in her pocket for her phone and a swear word did escape her lips this time. Her phone was on the counter in the kitchen where she'd thrown it before she'd picked up Mutt's leash.

"A...B...C..." Her breath caught as she ran toward the person. "Or is it C...A...B?"

All she could remember from the first aid course that Blake had insisted that the staff complete each year was the first two words...circulation and breathing. Or was it airway and breathing? Even as she tried to remember the sequence, a memory flashed through her mind. Damn, she couldn't even remember the funny song she'd made up at the course. She'd changed "shake and shout" into "twist and shout" and had performed an impromptu dance with the mannequin. All she could remember was the rest of the staff rolling around with laughter at her little performance. Blake had glared at her before his lips had twitched, too, and he'd given in to laughter. Now Georgie racked her brain for the rest of the words. She'd never had to administer first aid. The guy—she was now close enough to see it was a man—was lying on his stomach with his arms stretched above his head and his face turned away from her. Georgie reached him, knelt down, and grabbed his shoulders to put him in the recovery position. She could remember that much at least—hopefully the rest of the first aid knowledge would follow.

"What the hell do you think you're doing?"

Georgie rocked back on her heels as the guy pushed himself up onto his forearms and turned his head to face her. A pair of ice-blue eyes stared into hers and a shiver ran down Georgie's spine as she sat back on the wet sand, and the shiver didn't have anything to do with the cold water that was seeping through her shorts.

Oh...my God. He's gorgeous. She exhaled a huge breath of relief and put her hand to her chest. "Oh, thank goodness. I thought you were drowned."

"Well, I'm not." His voice was short, and Georgie narrowed her eyes. A trickle of blood was running down his cheek.

"But you're hurt."

He rolled over, sat up, and looked away from her. "No, I was just catching my breath." She sensed that every word he spoke to her was done so reluctantly. "So thank you, you can go now. Your dog's waiting for you."

Mutt had bounded over to see what was happening and stood next to Georgie as he shook the water from his coat, spraying her with drops of cold water.

"Your head's bleeding. What happened?" She reached out to touch his face, but he leaned away from her reach.

"I told you, I'm fine." His voice was rude, and he scowled at her, his expression grim.

"Well, get up and show me you're okay." Georgie pushed herself to her feet, put her hands on her hips, and stared down at him. He had longish hair plastered to his head, and despite being pale and gaunt, his face was beautifully proportioned. His clothes were soaked and stuck to his body; a pair of black shorts clung to long muscular legs and a sleeveless white T-shirt showed off a set of well-toned biceps.

"What about your kayak? If you're all right,

are you going to get it before it floats away?" She wasn't convinced that the guy was okay, and even if he was angry at her for some reason, she wasn't going to leave him until she was sure. He frowned at her before looking out to where the kayak was now bobbing in the small swell.

"Damn." He tried to stand but grabbed his head and sat back down.

Georgie gestured for him to stay sitting. The blood was trickling down his neck now. She called to Mutt and the dog walked over quietly, as if sensing there was something wrong.

"Sit." She pointed to the sand next to the man. "Stay."

Heading into the break, she gasped as the cold water hit her bare thighs and she waited for the wave to recede. The kayak was floating in waist-deep water, and when the surge pulled back, Georgie grabbed the end of the small craft and dragged it to the shore. It slid up the wet sand with a harsh grinding sound, and she pulled it up as far as she could, away from the rising tide.

"Leave it." The voice was peevish.

Georgie turned and glared at its owner as she dropped the kayak. She put her hands on her hips and stood over him. "I don't know who you are, mister, but here in Hideaway Beach, we do the neighbourly thing and look out for someone who needs a hand."

By the time she'd finished speaking, he'd pushed himself to his feet and she took a step back to look up at him. She was tall, but he towered over her and stared at her before she dropped her gaze and turned away.

"Come on, Mutt. It's time for us to go home."

She shot him a final look to make sure he was still standing before she headed toward the path, through the orange grove, and back to the cottage, Mutt close at her heels.

##

House-sitting the cottage for her friends until she left for Hawaii was opportune, as Georgie had given up the lease on her small apartment in Maleny. She had also offered to look after Ana's pets, Mutt and Sooky, the cat, while she was there, and the owners of the cottage had had no problem with that. Mutt was supposed to be going into town to stay at Uncle Renzo's house until Blake and Ana came back from Melbourne in the spring, but until Georgie left he could stay by the beach and Sooky could also stay with someone she knew. Now Sooky wrapped herself around Georgie's legs, meowing for her dinner. Georgie threw Mutt's leash onto the table on the porch. By the time she'd walked up from the beach the sun had set, and she flicked the light on after she opened the door.

She couldn't get the guy on the beach out of

her head. Maybe she should have stayed with him, no matter how rude he'd been. There was no sign of a car anywhere along the road. He could have paddled for miles before he'd come ashore.

With a shrug, she tried to put him from her mind. That was the old Georgie; always the worrier, always the caretaker of everyone's feelings and well-being. The new Georgie, with strong resolve and thick skin, would forget all about him and let him look after himself. She'd always hated confrontation, but her soft side would have given in and she would have stayed to see if he was okay, no matter what he'd said.

Yes, that's a big step forward. Turning my back on him and leaving him to look after himself.

Brent's comments had toughened her up. Knowing that he had used her sealed Georgie's determination to change. Supposedly, what didn't kill you made you stronger, so now she was a new, stronger Georgie. No more looking after guys in need. Mr. Kayak Paddler was her first test. Okay, she'd sort of rescued him—but now he could go it alone.

No longer was she going to try to make everything right for everyone.

And I passed with flying colours.

Now for an early night, to get ready for an early start at the house next door, while she worked up the courage to take on her trip around the world.

I can do it. But the last thing to flit through her mind as sleep claimed her was a gaunt, unshaven face with ice-blue eyes.

Chapter Two

Liam sneezed and put his hand up to his forehead as he felt the pull on his skin. His hand came away smeared with a streak of blood. The small wound had begun to bleed again. He'd managed to staunch the slow bleeding last night once he'd climbed the hill, stripped off his wet clothes, and showered, but he'd ended up with a raging headache. Now he swung his bare legs over the side of the bed and sat for a moment until the throbbing eased. Then he pulled on his jeans and padded barefoot down to the kitchen.

He rummaged in the medicine cabinet above the stove and found some of the Panadol he'd unpacked a couple of days ago. He swallowed two and chased them down with a large glass of water. Standing there for a moment, he debated whether to put the coffeemaker on or go back to bed. A shiver ran through him as he registered the chill of the cold tiles beneath his bare feet. He glanced up at the clock and sighed. It was close to seven o'clock and it wouldn't be long before the restoration company arrived to start work on his bookshelves. He had to get to the computer today. He couldn't afford to let another day slip by without putting some words on paper—or screen.

After he put the coffee on, Liam crossed to the window and looked out over the ocean. There was not a breath of wind, and the silver sheen of the calm water soothed him. Nothing moved; the trees were still in the quiet before sunrise, and there was no birdsong. He'd been relieved to only occasionally hear the dull roar of traffic when the wind blew from the west, but he had been dismayed last night to see lights on at the house next door. It looked like there was someone in it. He'd avoid them and keep to himself.

The last thing he felt like doing was being neighbourly. This house was perfect for him. He grinned to himself. Okay, he might be too young, but he saw this cliff top house as his place to settle and be happy as a recluse. He'd had enough of travelling and the experiences that went with it. He was here on the Sunshine Coast to stay. If the neighbours thought he was a hermit, that would suit him just fine.

That thought reminded him of the woman down on the beach last night. He knew he'd been rude, but overturning his kayak had been a stupid, careless thing to do, and he'd been angry at himself. When she'd tried to help, it had been the last straw, and she'd borne the brunt of his ill temper. It was bad enough that she'd retrieved the kayak while he'd lain on the sand. He hadn't needed her to administer first aid to him. God, he was lucky she hadn't tried mouth-to-mouth on him. Even though he'd told her he was okay, the headache this morning was bad enough to make him suspect he had a touch of concussion.

A flash of bright colour along his fence caught his attention and he leaned forward and peered through the glass. Damn, it was almost as though he'd conjured the woman up. He stepped back into the shadows as the woman from the beach followed the dog along the back of his fence line. He'd discovered who lived in the house next door. She was dressed in jeans today, with a long-sleeved red-and-white-checked shirt hanging loose over them, and a small bag slung over her shoulder. The red in her shirt clashed with the deep auburn hair he'd noticed yesterday. He waited for her to turn onto the beach trail, but she headed for his back gate. The clang of the metal latch told him she was coming onto his property, and he groaned.

What the hell is she doing here and why so early in the morning?

He definitely was not feeling neighbourly this morning.

***

As Georgie opened the gate to the house next door to the cottage, an unfamiliar ripple of fear ran through her.

Alone. It had been almost two years since

she'd last been out on a building job, and back then she'd always had Sienna and Ana with her. Since the three girls had sold their restoration business and gone their separate ways, she'd worked in the office of Blake's hardware store. Ana had settled down to look after her new baby and Sienna had immersed herself in her sculpting and her gallery in Noosa.

Now Georgie stood inside the gate and took a deep breath as she curled her hand in Mutt's fur. He put his head against her leg and looked up at her with his deep brown eyes.

Alone, completely alone. And she knew it wasn't just the experience of being alone on a job that was making her legs tremble. It was accepting that being alone in life was what she wanted. It was the decision she'd made. What she'd pushed herself into in the last two months finally hit her as she stood outside this dark, forbidding house. She was similar to her mother. Marietta had pretty much died alone, and it looked like her own life was going in the same direction. Her mother had been unhappy, but that wasn't going to be Georgie's way.

I am going to be positive about my life alone. It wasn't about being alone; it was about independence, and she would embrace it. No more mooning about for her. No more men to make her life complete.

It was certainly not a prediction any of them

would have made a few years ago. The standing joke among the three friends had been Georgie's determination to get married and live the suburban dream.

Who would have imagined their current situations? Ana had Blake and their gorgeous little baby, Faith. Sienna was madly in love, settled into domestic bliss and running the gallery with Jack, her artist partner.

And here am I. Not alone…just independent.

"You are such a coward, Georgie Sacchi." She fought back the tremble in her legs and took a deep breath as she gripped the gate with shaky fingers and pulled it shut behind her with a firm click. "Get over it. That is your new mantra. Forget 'it's not you, it's me.' From now on it's going to be, 'I value my independence.'"

As she looked around, her muscles slowly relaxed and the panic began to subside. The sun cleared the silver ocean to the east, and a glimmer of confidence filtered through her as the early-morning sunlight hit the water of the Pacific Ocean. The water was a mirror of unruffled silver this morning, and it calmed her. She swallowed and headed around the house to the front door of the old mansion. She and the girls would have loved to have gotten their hands on this place when they were in the restoration business, but old Mr. Humphries had hung on to it until he'd died. When the house had finally gone on the market, it had sold within a week. No one even knew who'd bought it.

All Georgie knew was that it belonged to some author who now wanted two whole rooms of bookshelves built. She'd dropped the contract off for Blake in Maleny a few weeks back.

She had no doubt she could do the job. She'd brought her tape to measure up this morning. After she did the measuring, she'd take Mutt back to the cottage and head into the hardware store to pick up the supplies to get started. Georgie let a grin cross her face; the new owner would soon find out there were a lot more jobs needed in the old house. It could keep her cousins, Tony and Johnny, the new owners of the restoration business, in work for years, if the man could afford it.

"Are you lost?" The deep voice pulled her out of her reverie, and she looked up at the open door and stifled a gasp. It was the guy from the beach. She hadn't even considered that he might be her new neighbour.

"You're still bleeding," Georgie said stupidly as the smile left her face.

She stared at him as he brushed his hand through his longish hair and pressed the pad of his thumb against the small cut. With his hair dry and some colour back in his face, he was even better looking than yesterday. The angles of his face, which had appeared gaunt and harsh in his pallor yesterday when his hair had been wet and plastered to his skull, now settled into high cheekbones that were accentuated by the dark stubble on his jaw. His light brown hair curled slightly and reached past the base of his neck, brushing his bare shoulders. Pale blue irises in almond-shaped eyes were fanned by long dark lashes, but his eyes were still as cold and unfriendly as they'd been yesterday. He had the most beautiful lips she had ever seen on a man, but they were set in a straight line.

"What do you want?" His voice was terse.

Georgie pulled herself together and closed her mouth as he stared at her. "I'm here for the, er…the job."

He ran one hand through his hair at the same time he eased the door closed. "Look, I've got no idea what you're talking about. And yes, I'm bleeding, and I have the mother of a headache. Good-bye."

The door shut in her face and she looked down at Mutt. At least her sad thoughts and panic had fled. She grinned and rapped on the door. Showing the rude man up was going to be enjoyable.

"Go away." Even when he was being rude, his husky voice sounded sexy.

She lifted her hand and knocked again and

waited. The door opened slowly, and he stared at her without speaking.

"Knock, knock," Georgie said.

"What?" Mr. Kayak Paddler frowned and put his hand up to his forehead.

Maybe the guy had a concussion?

"You're supposed to say 'who's there?'"

"Who's there?" Gritted teeth and not even a glimmer of a smile.

"The bookshelf."

"The bookshelf who?" There was a tiny twitch at the corner of his gorgeous mouth.

"The bookshelf builder. I am here"—Georgie enunciated each word clearly—"to build your bookshelves."

"What?" The look on his face was priceless, and any sympathy she had for his injury had disappeared.

"I'm from BB Hardware. You ordered two rooms of bookshelves to be built?" She grinned down at Mutt when he supported her with a loud bark.

"Yes. Yes, I did." The hunk holding the door looked from her to Mutt and frowned. "You're the handyman?"

"Yes, I'm the tradesperson. That's correct." Georgie held out her hand as she bit back the nasty retort that had sprung to her lips. Brent had had a problem with her doing a "man's job," as he'd called it

"Now let's start again. I'm Georgie Sacchi and I'm here to measure for your bookshelves."

He looked at her through the open door and scratched his head, ignoring her outstretched hand. Georgie kept her eyes away from his bare chest.

"So? Are you going to let me in…or don't you want the job done anymore?"

"Yes, of course I do." He opened the door a little and she took a step forward. "Where's your car?" The frown was deepening the furrows at the top of his nose. "And why did you bring the dog?"

"My car is at the cottage and I knew if Mutt saw me come over here without him, he'd howl all day."

"The cottage?"

"Look, are you sure you don't have a concussion from your accident yesterday?" It was time to take control. "Hold that door open. I'll be back in a minute." She grabbed Mutt's collar, led him around to the back of the house and opened the gate to the small garden. There was a bowl beneath the garden tap, and she filled it with water. She took a quick look around to make sure nothing had changed and that the garden was still secure before she closed the gate behind Mutt and hurried back around to the front door.

The door was wide open but there was no

sign of Kayak Man. Georgie took a hesitant step inside and called out. "Can I come in?"

She waited, but all was quiet. Taking a tentative step toward the hall, she looked around and shook her head; the place was in even worse condition than she remembered from her last visit here.

The sound of running water drew her to the kitchen. She'd visited here with Ana when they used to drop meals off for Mr. Humphries when he'd been homebound, and she knew her way around the place. Kayak Man stood at the sink holding a small cloth to his head.

"The blasted cut won't stop bleeding." He threw her a look, but she couldn't read his expression.

"Sit down." She pointed to the stool at the breakfast bar. "Where's your first aid kit?" She might have forgotten how to do CPR, but she was more than capable of putting a Band-Aid on a wound. He lifted his head and those piercing blue eyes held hers for a moment before he inclined his head to the left and winced. "There's a small plastic basket in the cupboard above the fridge."

Georgie walked across the kitchen and opened the cupboard he'd indicated. The basket was at the front of the shelf, and overflowed with boxes of bandages, tubes of lotion, and packets of medication. She dug through until she found a box of small circular bandages. "One of these should do the trick."

He sat on the stool as she'd directed, but if the look on his face was any indication, he wasn't at all comfortable with the *handyman* administering first aid.

She picked up the Band-Aid and walked slowly around the counter. "The quicker you let me do this, the sooner I can get to work and leave you in peace."

Georgie ripped the Band-Aid open. The snap of the plastic filled the uncomfortable silence in the room. She looked down at the bandage as she peeled the adhesive cover from the back, without once looking directly at him. "What's your name? The guys at the store didn't tell me, and I haven't collected the job sheet yet."

She grinned. *I'm not going to tell him I call him Mr. Kayak Man.* The expression on his face gave little hint of a sense of humour.

"Liam. Liam Wyndham." At least he answered her. The name was familiar, but she couldn't place it.

Deftly, she reached out and lifted away the small towel he had pressed to the wound. The cut was small and surrounded by a deep blue bruise. Georgie's legs went to jelly. As much as she was acting as though she could do this, she looked away from the jagged sides of the cut, which was still slowly seeping blood.

"You did a good job on yourself there. That's a nasty cut and you have a spectacular bruise. Do you think you should go to the hospital?"

"No." He reached his hand out. "If you can't do it, give me the Band-Aid and I'll put it on."

"I can do it." She leaned forward and tried to concentrate on placing the bandage carefully across the wound without getting the adhesive edges on the broken skin. She ignored the warmth from his bare shoulders as she leaned over him.

"There, that's it." She looked at his forehead and waited for a minute. The uncomfortable silence stretched between them and he kept his gaze averted. "There's no sign of fresh bleeding."

Liam pushed himself up to his feet and turned toward the door on the far wall. "Follow me."

And that's all he said, not even a thank-you. She followed him down the hallway, up two flights of stairs, and across another small hall before he stopped outside a set of solid carved double doors.

"This is going to be my office."

He flung open the door and stepped into the room without checking to see if she was behind him. Despite his injury, he'd taken the stairs two at a time and she'd had to hurry to keep up. The room was huge, and she spun around slowly, looking at the bare plastered walls.

"So where do you want the shelves?"

"All around." He gestured with a sweep of his arm.

"On every wall?" She knew she sounded sceptical. It was a huge room that Joe had used as a spare bedroom. The room was bigger than the apartment in Maleny she'd just vacated.

"Yes, and butting right up to the side of both the windows." The windows were large and pushed out and there was a magnificent view of the ocean from this side of the old house.

"How high?" She waited for his answer, knowing what he was going to say before he answered.

"To the ceiling."

"It's a very big job."

"If it's too much for your firm, I'll get someone to come down from the city." He went back to the entrance and stood in the doorway with his arms folded, leaning on the doorframe.

"No, there's no need to do that. It's quite within the scope of the store." Georgie pulled out her tape and walked across to the far side of the room. "Some of the walls may need reinforcing to carry the weight of shelves to the ceiling."

A look of astonishment crossed his face, as if

he was surprised that she knew what she was talking about. "So you do the measuring, and the builders come in and do the job?"

"No, Blake—the owner—asked me to do this job."

"Why? Because you live next door? You are a builder?"

"Yes, despite being a woman, I am a builder, and Blake asked me because this sort of job was—is—my specialty." Irritation at his obtuseness burned in Georgie's gut and she stared at him, waiting for him to come up with some sexist remark. "Living next door is purely coincidental—and temporary. So don't worry, I won't be bothering you."

Why the heck she'd said that she didn't know. Georgie slipped a professional mask over her face, tucked her tape into her jeans pocket, and turned to him. "Working with wood and creating features that match the age of the house is part of the restoration work that I've done for the past few years. I was in partnership with two others in our own company, and I'm very good at what I do. If you want to see my work, I can give you some addresses to check out." She pulled out her notebook and her pencil. "Now, while I measure up, I want you to think about what you want."

"I want bookshelves."

"What sort of bookshelves?"

"Ones that hold books." If he hadn't been scowling at her, the conversation would have been comical. Like something from a comedy sketch.

"Heavy books? Light books? Big books? Little books? Encyclopedias? Paperbacks?" Georgie refused to let him bother her and she grinned. "They certainly won't hold e-books."

"Ah, a comedian. Just what I need." He scowled at her. "Just book books."

He is so rude. She hoped he would stay out of her way while she was working here. It was such a big job; it would certainly fill up the whole month before she left on her trip.

"Fancy edges? Deep shelves? Different heights? And isn't there a second room on the order, too?" She stared at him and tapped her pencil against her notebook.

God forbid. This room alone was going to take a few weeks' work. There wouldn't be time for her to do both rooms, but she'd call Blake and sort that out later.

"Just this one will do, for the time being." He was obviously going to check her work out before he got her to do the second room. Georgie shrugged and turned away from him. Didn't matter, she wouldn't be around to do it, anyway.

Distant, aloof, and totally full of himself. It was a shame Blake and Ana would have to put up with him for a neighbour when they came home from Melbourne. He was very different from sweet old Joe Humphries.

Georgie wondered what sort of books this Liam Wyndham wrote and why he'd moved to the coast to write them; his name had rung a bell, but she couldn't place him.

The only thing she knew about him was his propensity for falling off kayaks in the ocean. He was in for a shock if he thought he could get away with keeping to himself in this community. She swallowed a grin. Maybe she would drop a hint to Thelma and Mitzi that there was a new person in town…well, almost in town. It wasn't that far to Maleny from the bay.

Focus. She turned her attention to the job in front of her.

"Okay, now I want you to think about what you'd like. You've hired a restoration firm through the store, so I'm assuming you want to keep it in line with the style of thc house." She straightened her shoulders and looked at him. "You don't want me to go and buy a set of ready-made IKEA bookshelves, right?"

He waved his hand, and his disinterest was clear. "Do whatever you think will suit the house. As long as it holds my books—of all shapes and sizes— I'll leave it up to you. I don't want to be disturbed.

I'll leave the front door unlocked each morning. There's a bathroom at the end of this corridor." His voice was short as he turned away from her. His final words reached her as he disappeared through the door. "Send me the bill when it's finished."

Georgie snapped her mouth shut. The ruder he was, the happier she would be. His amazing good looks were at such odds with his personality that the attraction that had initially tugged at her was doused with cold water. And to completely kill it, all she had to do was remember her new mantra.

I value my independence. Georgie grinned. It was getting easier every time she thought the words.

It was of no concern to her that this guy looked like a film star. She needed no man…and this rude guy who wanted bookshelves would get just that and no second thought or consideration from her. If she could let herself in and out each day and pretend he wasn't around, that would suit her just fine. She would do the job and prepare herself for her big adventure. The size of the job would help. She'd have no time to worry about Mr. Kayak Man, and get the shelves done before she set off.

Hmmm. Liam. Nice name. Suits the good looks.

Georgie shook herself and pulled out her measuring tape.

Chapter Three

Liam leaned back in his chair and looked around the small room he'd set up as his temporary office. The desk was clear, apart from the laptop computer; his essential reference books were in a box on the floor within reach; and the bulletin board was covered with glossy photos from Nepal. The floor in this room had a slight slope to it, and there was an ominous crack in the moulded arch above the door.

He'd known when he'd bought the place that it was in need of repair, but the location had appealed to him. Knowing it from his childhood had also brought a measure of security with it. Private and perched on top of the cliff overlooking the bay, it reminded him of some of the houses from Alfred Hitchcock movies. He'd hoped the mysterious atmosphere would feed his muse.

What he hadn't factored in was that if the house was to be restored—and repaired—there would be a constant stream of workmen—or women, God forbid—through the place. So much for living the life of a recluse. This morning he was blaming the presence of his redheaded rescuer for the desertion of the muse. No matter that he hadn't been able to write for months. Today, he knew that someone else was in the house, and she would likely come around when she'd finished measuring up, even though he'd told her not to bother him. Waiting for the inevitable interruption was wreaking havoc with his *concentration.*

It was. That's all it was. Once the redhead was gone for the day, he'd get some words down. He looked at the blank document on the monitor in front of him and it caught his reflection, and his eyes stared back accusingly at him.

I give up.

Liam pushed himself to his feet with a grunt and blocked all other thoughts from his mind as he crossed to the window and looked down at the untidy backyard.

Another job that needs doing. He'd deliberately set up this room as his study because it had no view over the sea. No distraction. The last thing he needed was to stare out over the water when he should be getting his word count up.

Ha. That's a joke. It was impossible to count words that were not written. As if on cue, his phone buzzed and he debated whether to answer it or not, especially when he picked it up and his agent's number flashed on the screen accusingly.

"Hello, Sarah." Liam stared down at the overgrown lawn below.

"Liam, where have you been? I tried to reach you all day yesterday."

"I was kayaking."

The silence on the other end of the phone relayed Sarah's displeasure. He knew he was letting her down, but somehow he'd get this book written as soon as he was settled in the house. He had to.

"So you've got some words down then? You're feeling better…the block is gone?"

Last month, he'd stupidly shared with her that he'd been suffering from a great dose of writer's block—ever since he'd come back from Nepal. It wouldn't hurt to stretch the truth a little to get her off his back. "Yeah, I have…and I am."

Liam straightened and brushed his hair back, accidentally knocking his head, and a deep throb winged across his brow.

"That's good then. Your new editor wants to meet you in Brisbane next Tuesday and have a look at the first few chapters." Sarah sounded a bit happier after hearing his white lie. He did have some words down. He'd thought of a title for this adventure story and typed it at the top of the first page. And he'd typed "Chapter One" below that.

Mustn't forget that. He ran his hand over the back of his neck as panic lodged in his throat.

"A new editor? Why do we have to meet? It takes time away from my writing." Liam frowned and the bandage pulled again. "And I'll have to hire a car. I haven't bought one yet."

"Yes, I know." Sarah's tone was patient, and he knew she was trying to placate him. But he also knew she was as hard as nails and would ride him until he finished the blasted book. Sarah had been with him since he'd shopped his first book around to publishers. She'd seen the worth in his story, taken a chance on him, and had sold it in a bidding war that had surprised both of them. Then she had celebrated with him when *Guardian of the Soul* had made *The New York Times* bestseller list two weeks after release. When he'd needed pushing, she'd been the one to do it.

And by God, he needed it now.

Sarah had also been a rock when Vanessa had died, and with Mike, her lawyer husband, had dealt with all the paperwork. Even though Liam and Vanessa had already separated, Liam had still felt as though he should look after the formalities of her death. Sarah and Mike had pulled strings and gotten him home from Nepal as quickly as they could. So he felt guilty about letting Sarah down now. He was her biggest client, and if this three-book contract went west, she stood to lose a lot of money, too. That thought had nagged at him for the past few days. Sarah and Mike were good people, and he was honoured to count them among his friends.

Ha. Probably my only friends. It was amazing who had disappeared after they'd read the crap about his marriage in the papers. None of his so-called friends had called him since he'd been back in Queensland. Not that he really cared. A private life with no socialising suited him and meant that he had more time to write.

"Do you want me to fly up from Sydney and come to the meeting with you?" Sarah's voice was soft and he hated lying to her. "You have been out since you moved up there, I hope? You're not turning into a recluse, are you?"

Sarah knew him too well. Liam chewed the side of his cheek as he stared down at the garden. The redhead's dog was stretched out in the warmth of the morning sun. A feeling of nostalgia ran through him. Big clumsy dogs had been a large part of his growing up on the farm. He probably should get a dog, now that he was settled. Vanessa had had one of those fluffy toy dogs and he'd hated the yapping thing. It was one of the many things they'd fought about before things had gone really bad. Crazily enough, when she'd finally left him and taken off with that other guy, he'd missed the dog more than he'd missed her.

"Liam? Are you there?"

"Sorry. No, there's no need to come." He turned away from the window and focused on the conversation. "I'll be fine. Just email me the details of the meeting and I'll be there."

"With your chapters?"

"Yes, with my chapters. Look, I have to go. I've got someone here measuring the house for some work for me." He used that as an excuse before Sarah could ask more specific questions about his progress. "Say hello to Mike for me. I'll let you know how the meeting goes. Bye."

He disconnected and put the phone in his pocket before Sarah could reply. With an impatient glance at the desk—any desire to write had completely disappeared now—he opened the door and headed outside for some fresh air.

***

Georgie frowned as she tucked the pencil into the back pocket of her jeans. The walls were out of alignment and she was going to have to find Mr. Kayak Man and talk to him about the design. She couldn't think of him as Liam—it was too soft a name for someone with his hard and implacable demeanour.

Liam—the name—should belong to someone kind and creative. An artist, although Sienna's Jack was an artist and Jack wasn't a name they would have picked for one. Georgie grinned as she stepped into the hall. She and Sienna had always thought up characters for guy's names when they were in their teens. Liam had been one of her favourites…and now it just proved her poor judgment. This guy was a sullen and rude jerk, not the soft and dreamy Liam of her teenage imagination.

Before she sought him out, she'd go down and check on Mutt. It had taken longer than she'd thought to measure, and she hadn't left him much water. At least he wasn't howling; that would really set the guy off. Apart from the creak of the stairs beneath her heavy boots, the house was quiet as she hurried down to the bottom level. There was no sign of Liam, and she put her notepad and pencil on the table beside the front door before she went out quietly, leaving the door half open so she could come back inside after she checked on Mutt. Her footsteps were quiet on the grass, and Georgie breathed deeply as she walked along the side of the house. A stiff breeze blew in from the sea, and the salt gave the air a sharp tang. She'd always loved it out here. The fragrance of the orange blossoms on the breeze was amazing.

If she did come back to the Sunshine Coast after her year away, she'd look for a place on the cliffs along this beach. Even after she paid for her air ticket, she still had a tidy sum put away from the sale of their restoration business, and the generous salary from Blake for working in the store office had added to it over the past couple of years. Her trip was going to be economical; she was planning a backpacking tour, much to her travel agent's dismay. The round-the-world ticket alone had cost her enough as it was, without going the five-star-hotels route. That way she'd save her money and have more options when the year was up. Nerves jangled in Georgie's stomach and she pushed away the thought of her planned trip.

Plenty of time to think about that.

As she neared the corner of the house, the muted tones of a soft voice reached her. She paused with her head tilted to the side and listened. It was coming from the backyard. She stepped forward quietly, put her arms on the gate, and looked across the unkempt lawn. Liam was sitting on the ground beneath the hanging branches of a large tree and had his arms around Mutt. His face was in Mutt's fur, and his voice was sad as he spoke to the dog.

"Just like you, boy." His words were muffled, but Georgie could make them out. She stepped back, feeling as though she was intruding on his privacy—and he'd made it quite clear he wanted privacy, no matter what.

"He was a good dog, my best mate, and he died." Before she could step back far enough, Liam lifted his head and looked out to the ocean, and the naked grief on his face slammed into her chest like a physical pain. She put her hand up to her mouth and took another step back before he could see her. Her foot rolled over on the edge of the path and Georgie gasped as her legs went out from under her. Her butt hit the ground with a solid thud, and her elbow hit an empty pot, which tipped over onto the path with a loud crash.

By the time she caught her breath and righted the pot, she was looking up into eyes that were dancing with amusement. The sadness on Liam's face had gone and she wondered if she'd imagined it.

He opened the gate and Mutt bounded past him and licked her as she tried to push herself to her feet.

"Are you okay?" His voice was *almost* kind as he held his hand out to her. She was pleased to see he'd put on a T-shirt and she didn't have to look at his bare chest any more. Georgie reached up for his hand and pulled herself up, dropping it as soon as she was on her feet. She brushed the back of her jeans and tried to ignore the heat that filled her cheeks.

What a klutz.

"Yes, I'm fine." She tried to keep her voice businesslike and brisk as her eyes met his. A warm, familiar feeling curled in her stomach as he stared at her. It had been dim in the kitchen, and she hadn't noticed the tiny smile wrinkles that fanned out beside his eyes, despite putting the bandage on his head. He was older than she'd first thought, and altogether too good-looking for her peace of mind. He was much easier to deal with when he was being rude to her.

"I was just coming to check whether Mutt had water before I came to find you. I didn't plan on making such a graceful arrival." Georgie chuckled.

One dark eyebrow quirked in a question and she rushed on. "I know you didn't want to be disturbed but I need to ask you about the design. There's a problem with the room."

Mutt slunk away from her toward the track to the beach, and she wagged a finger at him. "Uh-uh, no beach today, Mutt." She reached out and grabbed his collar. "I'll just check he has water and I'll meet you up there. Okay?"

"It's okay. He can come inside with us. I'll get him a bowl of water on the way through the kitchen." Liam reached down and patted Mutt's head. "He's a friendly dog. How old is he?"

"I'm not sure. I'm only minding him for a friend before I—"

Liam looked at her curiously as he walked beside her along the path to the front door. "Before you what?"

"Before I go away."

"Where are you going?"

Where had the taciturn man from this morning gone?

"I'm going on a holiday." She wasn't going

to share all her personal business with him.

"And so what happens to Mutt then?" Liam stood back and gestured her through the door in front of him. Mutt pushed past as though he belonged inside. "Where will he go?"

"He goes to my uncle's house until my friends come home. I'm minding the house—and Mutt for my other friend—while I do your job. And Sooky the cat." She swallowed and followed him to the kitchen. Chatterbox, wear-her-heart-on-her-sleeve Georgie was back and telling the world her business. God, she could feel the blush stealing over her cheeks.

Now close your mouth and stop blabbing.

Liam opened a cupboard and pulled out a plastic container. She watched as he crossed to the sink and filled it with water before placing it on the tiled floor for Mutt, who took a big slurping drink and flopped down.

Georgie frowned at the dog and muttered beneath her breath. "Make yourself at home, why don't you."

"He's fine."

"Thank you." She turned to the door. "Now are you interested in listening to me this time?" Again, she pulled out her brisk, businesslike voice. Being in Liam's company was starting to unnerve her, especially now that he was being a bit more hospitable. She wanted to appear calm, and not gab all her private business just because he was acting like a reasonable human being. She deliberately pulled an image of Brent's face into her head to remind herself of her determination to stay distant, and not allow herself to be attracted to any man, and especially not this one, just because he'd been pleasant to her friend's dog.

He levelled a cool gaze on her. "If I have to."

Good, the difficult Liam had returned.

Chapter Four

Liam stood back and allowed Georgie to precede him up the staircase. He'd noticed the moment when she had gone quiet on him. Her whole demeanour had changed and it had been strange to watch. Uncertainty had crossed her face while she'd told him about going away, and the brisk tradesperson had disappeared. Now, a woman with a distinct lack of confidence walked ahead of him.

He pushed away the surge of interest. That was the writer in him, always interested in people and their lives and their personalities, and in one way, he welcomed the feeling. It was the first sign of his muse that had appeared in weeks. On the other hand, he didn't like the response his body was having to the sight of her shapely derriere moulded by snug-fitting jeans as he followed her up the staircase.

She'd knotted the long work shirt at the front of her waist, and her red hair was scraped back into a high ponytail that swished in front of him. The colour of her hair fascinated him. He'd never seen anything like it. It wasn't auburn and it wasn't red, it was more like a deep golden copper, and he wondered what it would feel like if he reached out and undid the ponytail and ran his fingers through it. Tucking his hands in his pockets, he followed her along the hall that ran the length of the top floor. They didn't speak until they reached the room at the end. Georgie opened the door and led the way in.

"So, what's the problem?" Liam glanced down at his watch and she compressed her lips, obviously getting the message he was trying to convey. The sooner she got out of here, the better for his peace of mind. He leaned against the door and waited for her to speak.

"I left my notebook downstairs by the door, but I don't need it. I'll be quick." She walked to the long wall at the back of the room and tapped her knuckles near the corner. A chunk of grey and white plaster fell and landed on the floor next to a few other pieces of similar size. "This bit will have to be knocked out and replaced before any shelving can be built onto it. It won't support the weight of the shelves, let alone when they are loaded with books."

"So do it." Impatience took over. He should be writing. Most of the morning had flown by and he hadn't written a single word. His desk was tidy, his pencils sharpened, and his email filed into folders. Another morning gone with nothing added to his story. This block had to crumble soon, but it certainly wasn't going to happen while he stood and listened to this far-too-attractive woman talking about knocking walls down in his house.

"And the—"

"Look. I appreciate that you want to share all this with me, but I don't really care how you go about it and what you have to do." Liam crossed his arms and kept his eyes on hers. "I want bookshelves. Just do whatever it takes." He flicked a dismissive hand, and he knew he was being rude, but the sooner he could go into the small room with his computer and lock himself away, the better. He was uncomfortable with his reaction to her. It had been a long time since he had taken pleasure in looking at a woman. Despite her old jeans and red work shirt, she had a sweet vulnerability that tugged at him.

He'd always been a sucker for a woman in need and look where that had gotten him.

But he did smother a grin as her voice followed him when he turned away and headed for the door.

"I'm sorry I bothered you. You'll get your bookshelves. Eventually."

A woman who always had to have the last word.

***

Mutt tugged on the leash, eager to get home when Georgie finished measuring up. Honestly, Georgie didn't know if she wanted to do this job or not. Maybe she should just forget it—leave for her trip and hand it back to the store.

But she'd promised Blake she'd do it, and she

knew he was worried enough about leaving the business in the hands of a manager while he and Ana were in Melbourne helping his old boss wind up his hardware business interests.

The wind had picked up and Georgie looked up at the scudding clouds. The weather was closing in and the temperature was dropping quickly. The look on his face as he'd buried his face in Mutt's fur came to mind and she hoped Liam wasn't planning on going out in the kayak today…and she was totally forgetting the tremble that had worked its way down her spine as he'd followed her up the stairs.

All men are off-limits. Even a sad-eyed rude guy who was drop-dead gorgeous. If he wanted to go out in his kayak, it was absolutely none of her business. She was not going to worry about him.

The sooner she got this job finished, the better. As soon as her vacation began, this uncertainty about leaving home behind would disappear and she'd have a wonderful time while she explored the world.

Who knows? Maybe she'd settle somewhere else and never come back to Hideaway Bay. There was a great wide world to discover and she was going to do it.

I am. Soon.

###

Backing out of the driveway in Ana's old

work ute was tricky. One of the side mirrors was hanging loose, and Georgie had to reach out and hold it steady as she steered with one hand. Georgie had sold her car before Blake asked her to do this job. Now she glanced across the seat and grinned. She'd thrown her notebook and tape on the seat and it had landed on a pile of papers. Ana's untidiness had driven Sienna crazy because she preferred everything in its right place. Georgie had teased her mercilessly when they were growing up. One sure-fire way to get Sienna hopping mad was to rearrange her shoes…or even better, hide one of a pair.

It had taken Georgie a couple of days to settle into the cottage and find everything she'd needed. But it was lonely—even with Mutt and Sooky to talk to. She fought back the surge of want that filled her throat, and the tears that pricked at her eyes. It was not to be for her, but she could still be happy that both Ana and Sienna had fallen in love and found their life partners.

The sun broke through the clouds as she parked the truck at the back of Blake's hardware store. The timber yard was empty and there was no sign of life. Her stomach grumbled and she realised she hadn't eaten since last night. This morning, she'd been keen to get next door to Liam's place and get the measuring done. Her coffee had kept her going for a while. Then she'd been too busy trying to ignore her reaction to the owner of the house to think of food.

Georgie sighed and headed out to the back street and walked along the small alley that brought her to Main Street. Since Blake had been the president of the local business organization, a few new shops had opened, and the tourist trade had picked up. She headed south toward Uncle Renzo's café and grinned as she spotted her surrogate aunt's pink Fireflite parked outside the new sweet shop. When old Joe Humphries had passed on, they'd all been amazed when he'd left the car to Mitzi. It had been locked away in his shed for years, and no one had even known it was in there. Everyone had been used to taking turns driving Mitzi and her sister, Thelma, around. It had been a surprise to learn that Mitzi was the holder of a driver's license that she had actually kept current.

Mitzi wouldn't divulge exactly why Joe had left it to her but hinted at a story. Now she was fast becoming a character as she drove the 1960 Fireflite to town each morning with her elderly sister sitting in the passenger seat beside her.

"Georgie!" Mitzi spotted her as soon as she stepped onto Main Street. The old lady was standing outside the sweet shop, dressed in her best clothes. A floral hat was perched on top of her soft white curls and an overflowing basket was balanced on her arm.

Georgie crossed the road and stepped up onto the high curb. She loved this town with its old-fashioned quirks, and she adored her elderly friends. It was going to be very hard to leave it behind when she set off on her adventure. A cloud of lavender enveloped her as she kissed the woman's soft cheek and took the heavy basket from Mitzi's arm.

"What on earth have you got in there? Have you been buying sweets?" Georgie lifted the red-checked cloth and peeked beneath. Bottles of lemon butter and small packets of fudge in clear cellophane tied with red ribbon filled the basket.

"We're going into business." Mitzi tapped her nose as she smiled at Georgie. "Now that we have wheels."

Georgie narrowed her eyes. "Business?" As well as not missing a trick, and being the district's busiest matchmakers, Thelma and Mitzi were full of moneymaking schemes that always seemed to fail.

"Yes. Thelma is inside negotiating now."

"Where?" Just as Georgie answered the question, the sweet shop door opened, and Thelma stepped out. Her smile spread even more as she saw Georgie standing beside her sister.

"What a lovely surprise and excellent timing." Tiny hands latched onto Georgie's arm and before she knew it she was being dragged into the shop. "Come on, Mitz, I've got us a sale."

Before she knew what was happening, Georgie had been introduced to the new owners of the sweet shop, Thelma had unloaded her basket onto the counter, and they were back out the door.

"Now we are going to have a celebration lunch." Mitzi held on to Georgie's arm. "And isn't he a nice young man?"

Georgie shook her head, not sure who Mitzi was referring to. "Who?"

"The owner of the sweet shop." Mitzi lowered her voice to a conspiratorial whisper. "That's his sister, not his wife."

Georgie rolled her eyes and grinned. "Ah, but you forget. I am leaving for my round-the-world trip on Christmas Eve. By myself. No time for a new man this week." She played along with them. They were well used to her succession of boyfriends and didn't need to know that part of her life was over. She'd done a great job of hiding the pain of Brent's breakup, and she was still cheerful and helpful Georgie to the world.

Thelma and Mitzi both frowned as they stared at her.

"We know, dear. That's what we're worried about. What if you meet someone on the top of one of these South American mountains? Why, we may never see you again." Mitzi's high-pitched voice trembled.

"I'll be quite safe."

"Oh, we're not worried about that. Well, don't get us wrong, we are, but what if you fall in love and never come home?" Thelma added her two cents.

"Of course I'll come home and visit you. And besides, I'm not going to fall in love."

Georgie let their chatter wash over her and gave the appropriate nods as Thelma put the empty basket in the boot of the car before they walked the short distance to Uncle Renzo's restaurant. She looked around, pleased to see the busy lunch trade. She missed Sienna and Ana so much. The three of them had often lunched here together when they'd been between restoration jobs and working in the hardware store before Blake had bought it.

Why did life have to change?

Renzo blew her a kiss as he put a plate of rolls in the middle of their table, and Georgie grinned back at him. He had been like a true father to her, when he and Lucia took her and Sienna into their family after Marietta had taken off.

"I have to be quick, girls." Georgie reached for the bread. The old dears loved to be treated as one of the gang. "I only came into town to get some timber for a job I'm doing for Blake."

Mitzi had a sad, dreamy look on her face and let out a little sigh.

"We heard you were working at Joe's old place." Thelma stared at her intently.

Georgie rolled her eyes.

Did nothing escape this pair?

But she did love them. They were like family to her.

"What's the new owner like? We must welcome him to town." Thelma's face brightened. "We could visit this afternoon and take him a cake!"

Mitzi clapped her old, gnarled hands. "Yes, we have plenty left from our market stall."

Should I be nice?

Georgie's better nature won out and she cleared her throat. "Mr. Wyndham, the new owner, seems to want to be left alone." How could she put it kindly? "I think he values his privacy and wants to keep to himself, so maybe give him a while to settle in."

"Of course he does, the poor man."

Georgie looked up from the roll she was buttering and frowned. "The poor man?"

"Yes, the poor man. Don't you know?" Thelma and Mitzi looked at each other and they both shook their heads. "Georgie dear, you do live in a little world of your own."

"Maybe I just don't listen to gossip." She knew her voice was sharp, and she immediately regretted it when Thelma's eyes clouded. "I'm sorry.

I just like to keep to myself."

Mitzi reached out and took her hand. "Oh, darling, we know how much you're hurting, no matter how much you smile. If I was brave enough to drive on that highway, I would chase that horrible Brent all the way to Brisbane and give him a kick in the bum"

Georgie couldn't help the peal of laughter that bubbled up from her chest at the thought of Mitzi kicking anyone in the bum. "Oh, I do so love you gals."

"You have to get over him," Thelma added.

Georgie swallowed and plastered a smile on her face. "I'm fine. You're worrying about nothing. I'm well and truly over Brent." She leaned forward and stared at Mitzi. "Okay, I know I'm going to regret this, but why is Liam a poor man?"

"His wife was killed when he was in the Himalayas."

"His wife? In a climbing accident?" No wonder Liam looked so sad.

"No, no, no." Thelma and Mitzi spoke together, and Georgie looked from one to the other. They were back in their element.

"*He* was in the Himalayas. She was killed in a car accident in Sydney," Mitzi said.

"The magazines said she was with her lover." Thelma shook her head from side to side. "That poor man. It's so hard to believe what they said, that he made her stay at home while he travelled around the world."

"Why would the magazines write about her? And him?" Slowly it dawned on Georgie that she'd thought his name was familiar. "I know he writes books, but I've never heard of him."

Mitzi sighed and gently shook her head. "Georgie, Liam Wyndham is a *famous* author. He was researching his next book when his wife died…with her *lover*."

Thelma leaned forward. "And the magazines said he'd stopped her from accessing their bank account before he went away. And changed the locks on their house. Of course, I don't believe a word of it. He looks like too nice a young man to do such a terrible thing to his wife."

"Oh, how sad." She closed her eyes and remembered the look on his face as he'd been with Mutt. "But you know what those magazines are like. They make most of the stories up just to sell more copies. I'm sure none of it's true."

"Well, she was killed, and we will go down to the coast and visit him tomorrow."

Georgie propped her chin in her hand and smiled at them, trying to divert the old ladies from their "welcome" quest. "I think that's very sweet but honestly, he's still unpacking. He barely had time to show me the room I'm building the shelves in. There are packing boxes piled up everywhere and he's obviously very busy." There was no need to tell them that he had found time to go kayaking in the ocean. "I know he doesn't want to be disturbed."

"Very well. Whatever you say, Georgie." They smiled sweetly at her.

##

It was mid-afternoon by the time Georgie had loaded the truck with buckets of plaster, a stepladder, and her tools, as well as a small amount of lumber. She asked the store to deliver the rest of the wood to Liam's house tomorrow.

Mr. Wyndham. Think of him as a client. Not the man with the sad life that Thelma and Mitzi had spilled the beans about. Now that she knew all that, she would keep them away from him. Not that her life was anything spectacular or worthy of gossip magazines, but she knew the pair of them would love to fill Liam in on her recent man trouble. And visit him they would, she had no doubt of that. She was really starting to regret confiding Brent's nasty words to Thelma and Mitzi. She should have known better, but Ana and Sienna weren't around anymore, and she'd needed a couple of soft shoulders to cry on. It was going to come back to bite her, for sure.

And all the more reason for her to keep her distance from Liam. He was ripe for the picking by the old, soft-hearted Georgie.

She was pretty sure she'd persuaded them to stay away, but knowing the pair of them so well, they were capable of anything to help a soul in need, especially now that they had *wheels*. A giggle bubbled up in Georgie's throat.

Oh, if only the world worked under their rules. A slice of cake and a cup of tea would solve any problem.

Georgie smiled as she drove Ana's ute up the drive to the old house. It was a good feeling to be back out and about to start a job. As much as she had enjoyed working in the store and doing administrative stuff, it was not the same as the hands-on work she loved doing—and was good at. Building, creating, and restoring old houses to their former glory was the best job ever.

This place was still Joe's old house to her, and it would be hard to start thinking of it as Liam's. She was hoping to slip in and unload the truck without being seen. He'd said he'd leave the door open for her, and he'd made it quite clear he didn't want to be disturbed. Georgie winced as she missed a gear with a loud crunch on the final bend before the truck rattled to a stop outside the front door.

Chapter Five

Liam shut down the computer, leaned back in his chair, and rubbed his eyes with the heels of his hands. At least the ferocious headache had gone. He'd spent a few hours clearing his email and changing the address for some of his bills. Then he'd read through his research notes and waited for inspiration to hit.

But nothing. Not one word, not one thought crossed his mind. The creative well was dry. He picked up a pencil and opened a fresh notebook. Maybe if he turned away from the computer the words would come. Concentrating, he gripped the pencil so tightly that it snapped in his fingers, and in disgust, he dropped it into the garbage pail next to the desk.

His heart skittered a beat as the crunching of gears sounded through the window. The interruption was welcome.

Georgie was back. The house had seemed empty since she'd left late this morning. Liam had not been able to help himself when she'd left. He'd stood at the window and watched her as she followed the dog down the hill to the cottage. She interested him and he wondered why she was living alone in someone else's house.

None of my business. But he still couldn't stop himself from pushing the chair back and crossing the room to the window. An old, battered ute was parked in the driveway. The truck bed was loaded with buckets, a ladder, a few lengths of timber, and a large toolbox. As he watched, Georgie opened the door and stood next to the truck. She looked up and he leaned out the open window.

"Would you like a hand?" He might as well help; there was nothing productive happening here. It was the polite thing to do and it had nothing to do with the warmth that ran through him when she smiled up at him.

"Yes, please. I won't refuse that offer." She waved and disappeared out of sight between the house and the truck.

Liam buttoned up his shirt and ran his fingers through his hair as he walked downstairs. By the time he opened the door, she'd unloaded half of the gear from the back of the truck onto the pebbled driveway.

"That was quick." He picked up two of the buckets and turned back to her. "You unload what's left while I carry it up. I assume it's going upstairs where you've been measuring up?"

"Yes, please, but you don't have to help me. I'm quite used to working by myself." Georgie held his gaze and a frisson of something ran down his back. He welcomed it; it was so good to feel. He knew he'd been in a state of numb disbelief since he'd come back from Nepal.

The buckets were heavy and the muscles in his arms were burning by the time he got to the top of the stairs. Despite telling Georgie he'd take everything up, she was right behind him, with a bucket in each hand. Liam put down the buckets he was carrying to open the door, and then stood back to let her past him into the office. Her shirt was still unbuttoned over her T-shirt, and he looked away from the soft swells beneath the close-fitting fabric. A lazy kick of something swirled through him as the fragrance of orange blossom drifted from her, and he pushed it away.

"I said I'd carry them up for you." His voice was short.

"You're the client. I'm the builder." She grinned at him as she put the buckets in the far corner and waited for him to carry his load through.

He should pick them up and stop standing there appreciating her curves, but it was almost impossible. He couldn't take his eyes from her, and he couldn't stop thinking about how gentle her fingers had been when she'd looked after his wound.

Liam clenched his hands around the bucket handle as determination filled him. *Push these feelings away; they are crazy.* He'd made a vow when Vanessa betrayed him. He'd fallen in love with her when he'd met her at a book signing and these same feelings had filled him when he'd first seen her standing in front of him, waiting to have her copy signed. Any pretty woman in a close-fitting T-shirt would elicit the same response.

Get over it.

"Put them over here in the corner. I'll go and get the tools." She passed him as he crossed the room, and he made a noise of assent in his throat.

They made four trips from the truck up to the office, but Liam made sure he took his time and that he was upstairs each time Georgie was down at the truck. He was already regretting helping and the feeling intensified when she came up with the final load.

"Thanks heaps for the help. You've saved me quite a few trips. Your stairs are killers."

Reluctantly, Liam turned from the window and looked at her. Her arms were full of assorted small packets of nails and screws that she clutched to her chest with one hand, and she had a medium-size piece of wood held beneath the other arm. He crossed the room and slid the lumber out, and his arm brushed her hand. When she dropped her head and her fair skin pinked up, he knew he was in trouble. What was it about Georgie that made her so easy to read?

Because whatever he was feeling, the feeling was obviously mutual. She was feeling it as well.

Holy hell. He had to get out of here before he

did something he'd regret.

He stepped away from her and put the wood down next to the buckets. The packs slid from her arms to the floor, and she crouched down, picked them up and pushed them into a small pile.

"So what's next?" He had to say something to break the tension in the room. He knew it wasn't just him, because something had flared in her eyes as she glanced up at him. He hadn't seen anyone look at him like that in a long time.

And I don't want to.

Georgie stood and smoothed her hands down over her thighs.

"Once my muscles stop screaming at me, I'm going to knock out the back wall." She put her hands up and twirled her ponytail into a knot on the top of her head before she reached into her pocket for a clip. Liam swore he could feel his blood pressure spike as her T-shirt strained against her soft curves.

"That'll be enough for today, and then when the truck brings the rest of the lumber tomorrow, I can start putting in the reinforcements for the shelves. They're cutting the timber to the right lengths for me since I've done all the measuring." She walked away from him and he stared at the back of her head and not at her shapely butt. "Then I'm going to—"

Georgie sat on the windowsill and kicked her

boot at the floor. "I'm sorry. I forgot you didn't want to know what's happening." She lifted her head and met his eyes squarely; her face pinked up even more. "Thanks for the help. I'll be fine now."

He waved his hand at her. "That's okay. I asked. I just wondered what was next."

"It's going to be very noisy while I knock that wall out. I hope it won't interrupt your work?" She chewed on her bottom lip, and he could tell she was ill at ease with him. She hadn't been like that before.

"My work?"

"I'll be honest with you. If you're going to live in this district, you'll soon find out nothing's private. I heard today in town that you're quite the celebrity and I put two and two together. But please don't think I was listening to gossip about you. With all these bookshelves"—his heartbeat kicked up a notch as a grin crossed her face—"I assume this is going to be your workspace and you're working somewhere else while you wait for this room to be ready?"

Liam was taken aback by her honesty, and he stared at her. Her eyes were clear as she held his with her steady gaze, and he could tell she was being open with him. In the world he'd become used to, no one ever came out and told the truth. There was no coquetry or game-playing in the way she spoke to him. And despite saying she hadn't been listening to gossip, she'd obviously heard all the stories about him. He looked away but he could still feel her stare fixed squarely on him.

"I thought you seemed sad, and now I know what happened, but it's none of my business, and if I can help or if you ever want to talk, just—" A strange expression crossed her face and she stopped talking and closed her eyes. "Shoot. Total rewind." She screwed her face up and clenched her hands in front of her eyes. "Please ignore every word I just said."

Liam opened his mouth, but before he could speak, she shook her head and pushed herself up from the windowsill.

"Look, I'm sorry." She brushed past him and for a moment he was tempted to reach out and pull her back. "I've changed my mind. I mean I've just remembered something I must do. I'll come back in the morning, and don't worry, I won't bother you again."

The sound of her work boots hitting the wooden stairs was followed by the slamming of the front door. Liam crossed to the window and watched as she drove off down the hill a lot faster than she'd driven up just a short time ago. He waited for her to turn onto her driveway, but the truck kept going, and she turned it onto the highway and headed south.

Maybe she had thought of something she had to do, and he'd read too much into the atmosphere between them. But it had been tense and for some reason he couldn't fathom why she'd taken off so quickly. And he hadn't even been rude to her. She'd been upset and that bothered him.

He tried to forget the way his body had responded to Georgie as she'd brushed past him, but more than that, the way he had reacted to the sadness in her expression when she'd babbled on about changing her mind. His heart had lodged in his throat as her eyes had widened and she'd stared at him.

Something was bothering her, and it was a good feeling to worry about someone else for a change.

***

For the first time since Brent had told her she was not marriage material and then had hightailed it to Brisbane with his new girlfriend, Georgie let her feelings out. She'd barely made it up the highway to the small beach where Uncle Renzo and Aunt Lucia had brought them to swim when they were small. Turning the ute into the small parking area, she was pleased to see there were no other cars there. The hot tears spilled down her cheeks as she killed the engine and it stopped with a noisy rattle.

God, she was so embarrassed and so stupid. One look at a man, and here she was offering to help him through his personal crisis. Mortification filled her as she remembered the words, she'd said to him.

68

If I can help...or if you ever want to talk.

A client. And not only a client, a famous author, at that. He must think she was an absolute idiot. He probably had a heap of friends and family, and here was the small-town builder offering to listen to his woes. She dropped her head into her hands and groaned.

It was so very tempting just to go back home, pack her bags, and leave. Georgie didn't want to face him again. In fact, she didn't want to see anyone she knew anymore. She needed to go away and try and find this independence she'd promised herself.

She pushed open the car door and stepped out into the cold wind. The chill was welcome because it took her mind off her problems for a brief moment as she crossed the parking lot to the wooden steps that led down to the beach.

The afternoon shadows lengthened as she walked along the wet sand. She had to get over this. It wasn't that she'd made a fool of herself and offered to listen to him that was the real problem.

Yeah, she was embarrassed, but being upset had more to do with the fact that she couldn't help herself.

Why? Why did she have to be so concerned about other people's problems? Every time she got involved with someone, it turned out badly. Sienna had always had her own theory about it. She said

Georgie was trying to be the mother she'd never had, and so she tried to mother everyone else in her life.

But that was rubbish. They'd had two mothers. The woman who'd given birth to her, and then Lucia who'd done a great job bringing them up after Marietta had run off and Uncle Renzo had taken them in.

So it had nothing to do with the way she'd grown up. There must be something lacking in her and she had to face up to that. She was just not meant to be in a relationship. Maybe it was because she tried too hard? Maybe it was because there was something missing in her character? More tears threatened as Georgie muttered, "Maybe I'm just unlovable?"

Maybe I should disappear and go and work in one of those African orphanages or something? But the thought of leaving the safety of the Sunshine Coast and all her friends in Maleny, and her family scared her half to death. Georgie knew she was firmly entrenched in her comfort zone and she didn't really want to leave it, no matter how excited she was pretending to be about this once-in-a-lifetime trip. It would probably be better to put the money it was going to cost for the trip into a house here at Hideaway Beach.

And forget about men, marriage, and the white-picket-fence dream the girls tease me about.

There was something about her that turned men away as soon as they got to know her, and Georgie knew she tried too hard to compensate for whatever it was. She looked up as a gust of cold wind came around the rocky point at the end of the bay, and realised it was getting dark. She turned around and walked slowly along the shore until the parking lot was in view again.

She let her thoughts settle on Liam and what she'd blurted out. Was it because of the attraction that had kicked in between them? She'd been aware of him watching her as she'd unloaded the truck. He was such a good-looking man and on top of that, his sadness had pulled at her heartstrings.

Why can't I just get on with my life, do the job that has to be done, and stay aloof? Independent.

She needed to take lessons from Sienna. No one could ever tell what she was thinking, and she pretended she didn't care about anyone. And she didn't spill her heart at the first opportunity, blab her business, and scare everyone off.

Now that she'd made a fool of herself, maybe he'd disappear, and she could put her head down and work as fast as she could. Get his shelves finished and get out of there.

Maybe she'd call Blake and see if he could find someone else to do the job. But she knew things had been tight since he'd taken over the store, and she didn't want to see the job go to a city firm because her cousins were booked up for months. So she'd honour her commitment.

Her mobile was ringing when she got back to the ute. Georgie reached for it and a wry grin lifted her lips when she glanced at the screen.

We might not be twins, but there is a connection between us.

"Hi, Sienna."

"Hey, sis."

A warm feeling settled in Georgie's chest and she laughed. "Don't you mean, hey, cuz?"

"No, we're sisters at heart. That's why I'm calling. I just had a feeling that something was wrong. You haven't called and I was worried about you. Is everything okay?"

Georgie hesitated. She and Sienna had always been completely truthful with each other…but now Sienna had Jack and she was finally happy.

Really happy. She doesn't need my problems.

"Georgie?"

"Yes?"

"What's wrong? I knew something wasn't right when you put your trip off for a month."

"No, everything's fine." Georgie hastened to reassure Sienna. "I've delayed my holiday as a favour for Blake."

"But you're still going?"

"Yes, I leave Christmas Eve." It looked like she'd managed to divert Sienna from the "are you okay" talk. "I'm going down to Brisbane to the travel agent on Tuesday to make the final plans on my itinerary."

"So what's so important about this job for Blake?"

"The guy who bought Joe Humphries's place is an author and he needs his office fitted out quickly. Tony and Johnny are on a big job at the moment and Blake asked me to take it on. He didn't want to lose the job to a city firm."

"Anyone we know?"

"No, I'd never heard of him. It's Liam Wyndham."

"Liam Wyndham! Are you kidding me? The same Liam Wyndham who wrote the Guardian series?"

"Yeah, I guess so."

"Georgie, have you been living under a rock? My God, he's huge. And he's living next door to you? I've got all his books."

Georgie knew something was coming by the tone in Sienna's voice. They might as well be twins. They could read each other like a book.

Very appropriate. She giggled softly…Sienna could always cheer her up.

"Do you think you could get him to autograph them for me?"

"No." Georgie could think of nothing worse than facing Liam again. "No way. I hardly see him. He's made it quite clear he wants his privacy and he'll be closeted in his study while I work." A hit of warmth ran up her neck as she remembered how she'd breached that privacy. "I tell you what you could do though, and you *might* get to see him. Mind you, only a very small *might*."

"What?"

"Are you busy this weekend? I could use some help. How would you and Jack like to come up to visit and you could do some fancy edges on a set of bookshelves for me?" If Sienna helped her out, she'd be able cut the job by a few days. And Sienna's work with wood was amazing. It would give the shelves that special touch to suit the old place. "I could do with some company, too."

"Suits me just fine. Jack's going back to Melbourne to sign for a commission in a building down there." The pride was evident in Sienna's voice and Georgie loved hearing it.

"I was thinking about a visit. And we can catch up and you can tell me what's wrong with you."

Georgie rolled her eyes. She thought she'd gotten away from that inquisition.

"I've got to take Jack to the Maroochy airport on Friday. I'll come to you after that."

"Girls' night in. Sounds good. Shame Ana's in Melbourne." Georgie was feeling happier by the minute. A gossip session with Sienna was just what she needed…as long as her cousin didn't pry too much into Georgie's feelings.

"Chill the wine," Sienna said.

"If you cook." Georgie laughed as they finalised their plans, and she threw her mobile onto the seat after they disconnected. The afternoon light was fading quickly by the time she backed the ute out of the small parking lot and turned onto the highway. Winter was taking a hold on the coast, but she'd soon be in a warmer climate. After that, who knew? In a way, it was exciting not knowing where she was going to go after Hawaii.

The walk on the beach and the conversation with Sienna had done her a world of good. Georgie took a deep breath. Tomorrow, she'd go back to Liam's and act like the professional tradesperson she was and pretend she hadn't been on the verge of tears and run out on him this afternoon.

She *would* be professional, and she *could* remain aloof.

Chapter Six

The best-laid plans flew out the window when Georgie shut the door of Ana's house behind her the next morning. She'd slept soundly, but late, and had deliberately left her starting time until midmorning so Liam would be settled into his study. She hoped that he'd left the front door unlocked as he'd promised, and she wouldn't have to face him. She'd have to see him sometime, but the later it was, the better prepared she'd be.

The delivery truck with the lumber for the shelves was due at eleven so she timed her arrival for then. He probably hadn't even noticed she wasn't there.

She walked up the hill, ignoring Mutt's mournful cries at being left behind. That was one less thing to be concerned about today. She didn't want to have to worry about leaving him in Liam's backyard.

One less opportunity for bumping into Liam.

She crested the small hill and groaned. Mitzi and Thelma's pink Fireflite was parked in the driveway outside Liam's front door and there was no sign of the truck from the store. The pebbled drive crunched beneath Georgie's feet as she debated whether to sneak upstairs and start work or acknowledge Thelma and Mitzi.

She'd kill them, she really would. Or she'd give them a good talking to about respecting people's privacy and turning up unannounced. Taking the cowardly option, she pushed the door open quietly and ignored the voices from the large living room as she tried to tiptoe across to the staircase. She frowned, trying to remember which step creaked.

"Georgie. Come in and say good morning to your *friends*."

Busted.

Liam stood at the door and she turned around slowly.

"They wouldn't leave until you arrived. Thelma and Mitzi wanted to say hello to you." His voice was cold and the implication that she was late for work hung in his words.

Georgie pulled herself up straight and tried to stare him down. She was her own boss, and he had no say in her working hours. A little spurt of anger stiffened her spine as she held onto the banister.

Good, embarrassment zero. Anger, one. Keep it together.

She raked a cool glance down his body and ignored the little jolt of her heart. He had knee-length chinos on this morning and his feet were bare. A loose white shirt completed the casual look and as she lifted her eyes to his face her heart thudded uncomfortably in her chest. It was just like the shirt

Colin Firth had worn in the famous lake scene that she and Sienna used to swoon over. His face was unshaven, and those sexy cheekbones were highlighted by the dark stubble. His ice-blue eyes held hers, but she fought the feeling that crept through her bones.

"All right. And then I have to get to work. The truck with the wood is due to arrive any minute."

"So that's why you're late?"

She stepped off the bottom stair and walked across the entry hall toward him, knowing there was a flush on her cheek. "Late?" She reached him and looked up into an amused gaze. *God, I wish the man would shave*, she thought irrationally. *The stubble just makes him better-looking.*

"I'm not late."

"I thought you had to knock the wall out?" His voice was low and there was dead silence from the living room. A grin pulled at the sides of Georgie's mouth as she imagined Thelma and Mitzi straining to hear their hushed conversation. Not hearing what she and Liam were saying would be killing them.

"I do." She let the grin take over and shot him a smile as she reached up and patted his shoulder. "You worry about your work and your guests, and I'll look after my work. Deal?"

Liam's arm stiffened beneath her fingers and

she knew he'd picked up the censure in her voice despite her sweet smile. She dropped her hand from his shoulder and pushed past him. Unfortunately, he was standing in the doorway, so she had to squeeze by to get to the living room. Every nerve ending stood at attention and her heartbeat picked up.

"Georgie." Thelma patted the sofa beside her. "We were worried about you, and so was Liam."

Liam? Already?

"You're very flushed, dear. You're not getting ill, are you?" Mitzi fluttered her little hands around.

"No, I hurried up the hill. I've got a delivery truck due at eleven. Now, don't you two have somewhere else you have to be? I'm sure Mr. Wyndham has some work waiting for him."

"It's all right. Liam knows you told us he was busy and that he didn't want to be disturbed. But he's such a sweet man. He said he was very happy to have us visit."

Georgie closed her eyes and took a breath. And she was sure they'd left nothing out about her, too.

"We had to come. There was a part from our car still in the garage here and we've been waiting for the new owner to arrive so we could come and get it."

"What part?" Georgie asked suspiciously.

She knew them too well. Apart from their craftwork and going to the markets, their day was filled with good-natured meddling and matchmaking.

"Oh, just a pink thing." Mitzi waved her dainty little hands again. "Liam is going to look for it on our way out."

Thelma smiled at her and Georgie bit back the sarcastic reply that was hovering on her lips. She looked up and was surprised to see a grin on Liam's face. Of course he'd picked up on what was going on. He could see right through this devious pair. She would be having stern words with them later.

"I'll go to the garage and see if I can find the pink 'thing.'" He walked over to the elderly pair and offered a hand to each of them to help them up. "And then I'll come back and give you a hand to unload the timber truck." He turned to Georgie as the elderly women picked up their bags.

"Oh, don't worry about the part now," said Thelma. "It wasn't urgent. We'll leave you and Georgie to wait for the truck. We'll come back and get it another day."

"Yes, it will give us a reason to come and visit again. We do love being neighbourly," Mitzi chimed in. "It's so important to make new residents of the coast feel welcome."

Georgie turned to Liam with a genuine grin this time. "And since Joe left Mitzi his car, they've been neighbourly everywhere.”

Georgie watched Liam as he escorted her two friends to the door. A tray with teacups and leftover cake sat on the coffee table and she grimaced. By the look of things they’d been here all morning.

Love it!

It didn’t matter. She’d made up her mind about how to handle Liam. She would ignore the nervous jolts and warm feelings that ran through her and get to work as soon as the truck was unloaded. Mitzi and Thelma’s being here when she’d arrived had broken the ice with Liam a little, although she still resented his comment about her being late.

“Oh, Georgie dear?” Georgie waited for what was coming as Thelma turned to her. “We’ve organised a little welcome reception for Liam at our place on Sunday.”

Mitzi piped up. “We’re having a garden party. You know how we love them.”

Georgie shook her head. “Sorry, gals, I can’t make it. I’ll be busy working here. And I’ve already welcomed Mr. Wyndham.” Her eyes met Liam’s and she could see the mirth in them.

What happened to the guy who wanted total privacy?

A welcome reception? He seemed pleased about it, by the grin on his face. Maybe she’d read him wrong. Maybe it was just her he didn’t like?

And unfortunately for her, he exuded even more hotness when there was a hint of a smile on his face. God help her if he actually smiled at her. She went weak at the knees just imagining it.

"Oh, but you have to come. Liam doesn't have a car yet and we've organised for you to drive him to our place."

Why did they always do this to me? She swore that Mitzi and Thelma had completed People Manipulation 101 right before they'd taken up Matchmaking 101. She tried to stare them down but they both quickly looked away from her and back to Liam.

"Come on, Liam. Help us into our car like the true gentleman you are, and we'll go back to town. If we leave now, we won't block the driveway for the timber truck. We'll come over and see your new office when it's finished. Georgie's work is magnificent."

"It's only a set of bookshelves; I'm not doing a full restoration." As soon as the words left her mouth and she watched Mitzi's face light up, Georgie wished she could pull them back.

"Oh, but you could. Joe's...I mean Liam's house is crying out for a touch like yours. You could do it instead of going—"

"Mitzi, I think Mr. Wyndham is waiting for you." Georgie clenched her fists by her side as she glared at her sweet old friend and kept her voice firm.

Mitzi walked to the car where Liam held open the driver's door. She turned her little wrinkled face up to him and a surge of guilt hit Georgie for thinking badly of them. They were just trying to be kind.

"Perhaps we could make you some frilly curtains," Mitzi said.

Thelma winked at her over the top of the car. Georgie snorted, and Liam closed the door, seemingly oblivious to the silent messages being passed around him.

***

Liam turned around to speak to Georgie as the huge old pink car drove sedately down the driveway, but she'd disappeared. He walked thoughtfully through the door and closed it quietly behind him as the sound of hammering began on the top floor.

So much for being a recluse.

He valued his privacy, and he'd come here just for that reason, but those dear old souls had managed to break through his barriers before he'd even had a chance to think. They'd bundled him into his kitchen, made a pot of tea, and produced a cake from a basket. He still didn't know which one was Thelma and which one was Mitzi. He'd barely managed to get a word in while they'd taken great delight in filling him in on all the locals around Maleny. There was enough new material filed away in his head to create a whole imaginary town populated with the colourful characters they'd described to him as they'd brewed tea and fed him cake. A little creative spurt niggled, and he welcomed it.

And they'd talked about Georgie. They'd hinted at a big secret but were loyal enough not to tell him anything private about her. It had whetted his curiosity. Maybe it would explain why he found her fascinating and so easy to read. He'd lost sleep last night worrying about what he'd done to upset her. It seemed as if she'd gotten embarrassed after she'd offered to listen to him if he wanted to talk. Then she'd run out and he'd let her go.

Kind. As well as interesting and beautiful. And a hard worker. He'd only known her a couple of days. She'd rescued him—or so she thought—retrieved his kayak, ministered first aid to him, and then turned up in dungarees and work boots. One of the most independent and self-contained women he'd ever met. Very different from Vanessa and her needy personality.

Before he went into his small study, he detoured via the kitchen and cut a huge slab of cake to take upstairs with him. He grinned; a spark of enthusiasm fired in his blood and it was unfamiliar. Ideas were turning into words in his head and he needed to get them down. He'd go up and see

Georgie after he was done.

A long while later, Liam stretched at his computer desk and looked around. The afternoon sunlight was pouring through the window and he was thirsty. He glanced down at the time on the bottom corner of his laptop screen.

"Damnation." He pushed the chair back and strode toward the door before cursing and turning back to his computer to save his work. The words had flowed, and he'd written the first three chapters of a new book.

Not the book his publisher was waiting for, but the story that had come into his head when he'd been listening to his visitors. Now he felt guilty that he'd locked himself away, and he'd completely forgotten about Georgie and the delivery truck. She would think he was the biggest louse around. He just hoped she hadn't carted the timber upstairs herself. After he saved his file, he headed for the door. The house was quiet. There was no banging, no sound of any work—he tipped his head to the side and listened. There was no sense of anyone in the house but him.

He strode along the top hall, listening as he made his way to the study. The door was closed, and he stood outside and tapped lightly on the heavy wood.

"Georgie? Are you in there?"

All was quiet as he pushed the door open. She'd gone but she'd obviously worked hard, and he'd heard none of it while he'd been in his creative zone. The back wall had been pulled down and piles of old plasterboard were sitting neatly in the corner. A new frame had been built, ready to support the shelves. Liam swivelled around and groaned. Four high piles of wood were stacked neatly beneath the window.

God, I hope she had some help to carry that up. Surely the truck driver would have helped. He'd apologise to her tomorrow.

For a moment, he debated whether he should wander down to her cottage now, but common sense won out. He wasn't going to go visit her for any old excuse just because he found her— Liam frowned. Why did he find her so fascinating? She was confident and independent and interesting. But that didn't mean he had to bother her.

Despite enjoying his visitors today, he still intended to keep to himself. He'd get Thelma and Mitzi's number from Georgie tomorrow, and take a rain check on the welcome. They'd sucked him in, and he'd agreed to come to their party but it was totally not his scene.

Too cosy for me. He valued his privacy too much to get involved with the townspeople.

They were sweet old ladies and although he'd

seen right through the reason for their visit, it had been kind of nice having company in his new house. Once he'd gotten on top of his book—the other one—he'd invite Sarah and Mike up for a weekend. Not a total recluse; just when it suited him.

It was time to start living again. *But slowly. Take it slowly.*

Liam crossed to the window and looked at the cottage down the hill.

Chapter Seven

It was Friday morning and Georgie cursed as she tried to lift the last length of wood into place. It was heavier than the rest and she had to get it up before she could start building the frame on the wall that joined this corner. She put the solid piece of lumber down, dropped to her knees, and caught her breath. It wasn't worth throwing her back out.

Looking around, she tried to figure out whether she could start at the other end of the window wall and wait till tomorrow, when Sienna would be here to help her lift the heavy piece of timber. In the meantime, she could set the joints at the corners where the two shelves would intersect.

She'd worked all week and hadn't laid eyes on Liam since Thelma and Mitzi had left on Tuesday. On the second day, she'd had a dreadful thought, worrying that he'd gone out in his kayak and tipped over again. Creeping quietly downstairs and through to the kitchen, a pile of dishes in the sink caught her eye. She put her hand to the coffeepot and breathed a sigh of relief as the warmth touched her skin. He wasn't far away. She could stop worrying.

Another day had passed, and Georgie had made great progress on the shelves. Occasionally, she would hear a door open and shut downstairs

beneath her on the wooden chair.

No, no, no.

She folded her arms in front of her on the old table and nodded mutely as his bare chest filled her gaze. She had known what a full-blown smile directed at her would do to her composure.

Pull yourself together.

"They were adorable. And the stories they told me"—Georgie rolled her eyes as the grin stayed on his face—"kicked off a spark for a new book and I've been writing ever since they left."

Georgie swallowed and tried to ignore the warmth filling her as he leaned close. This was an entirely different Liam from the one she'd been dealing with.

"I wasn't sure you were okay about them." She cleared her throat. "I'll have a cold drink, after all." Anything to take her attention away from the bare chest that filled her vision.

"Are you all right?" Liam reached out and put his hand on her arm and more heat surged into her cheeks. God, she'd be as red as a fire engine soon.

"Yes," she said slowly.

"I'm sorry I didn't help you unload the truck the other day." His fingers stayed on her arm as he looked at her. "Oh, no, I didn't expect you to. Troy, the driver from the store, carried most of it up for me while I was working." She moved away a little and

Liam lifted his hand from her arm.

"I was worried that you were angry with me because Thelma and Mitzi had turned up unannounced," she said.

"Even if I had been upset by getting interrupted, it wouldn't have been your fault. You didn't invite them." Liam narrowed his eyes thoughtfully and she felt like a butterfly pinned to a board. "And besides, they are a delightful pair."

Georgie slipped the tip of her tongue out and licked her dry lips, immediately regretting it as his gaze dropped to her mouth.

"Someone's done a real number on you, haven't they?"

"What?" The word came out as a squeak.

Liam ran a hand through his hair and tucked the loose bits behind his ear. "When you're not blushing, you're apologising, and I noticed the other day when the old dears were here, you were trying to make everything right."

He leaned back in the chair and sipped his coffee. Georgie stood and crossed to the sink and threw a glance over her shoulder as she filled a glass with water from the tap.

"So what makes you the expert?" He'd hit way too close to the bone, and she swallowed hard. "Do you write psychology books, too?"

"No, I'm a writer. I observe people and I've

become pretty good at figuring out what makes them tick."

Georgie drained her glass and put it in the sink. "Well, what makes me tick is the job that's waiting upstairs and the time clock that's ticking away." The sudden hurt that lodged in her chest took her breath away. She knew what was wrong with her. She didn't have to have some too-good-looking, pseudo-psychoanalyst writer look at her with his sexy eyes and put it into words. "My time goes on your bill and the sooner I get this job finished, the better."

His was still looking at her intently and she shifted from one booted foot to the other, uncomfortable beneath his stare.

"For both you…and me," she added.

"Look, I'm sorry if I overstepped the mark. I didn't mean to hurt your feelings."

"You've got me wrong, Liam. I've been trying to stay out of your way to preserve your precious privacy." Georgie waved a dismissive hand. She could act with the best of them. "And yes, I do have fair skin and I can't help it if I blush a lot. It's my complexion…nothing to do with my feelings." She strode to the door and casually flicked her ponytail with her fingers. "Matches the hair.

Her legs were shaking as she walked up the stairs. Just when she was enjoying the work and getting her head together, he had to remind her of how she always tried to smooth the way for everybody.

Okay, so I used to try to make everyone happy, but that's the old Georgie.

Get this job finished and then she'd be out of here. She'd take off into the big wide world and worry about no one but herself. The new, confident, look-after-herself Georgie would face life head-on and enjoy every minute of it.

I will.

She picked up the hammer and began knocking down the only wall left intact. A few minutes belting at the plaster had a soothing effect and she put the hammer down and wiped the perspiration from her brow. A light breeze was blowing in from the sea and she walked across to the window and let the cool air play on her damp skin.

When Sienna arrived tonight, she was going to unload on her. If she talked the whole Brent thing out, maybe she'd get over it quicker. That's what sisters were for. Though now they weren't real sisters—she'd never get used to that—they were still sisters in spirit. God, here she was on a trade job, building bookshelves for a man—okay a really, really good-looking man—and she was turning it into an emotion-fest.

Georgie knew she was overreacting. And the

feelings brought to the surface by overthinking the guys who'd dumped her had made her more vulnerable to yet another good-looking man. And now the usual sequence of events was starting all over again.

Fall for a man.

He leaves.

Broken heart.

Move on.

Okay, maybe she was exaggerating. They hadn't all dumped her. She'd broken a few of the relationships off herself. But with Brent, she just hadn't seen the end coming.

A good dose of Sienna reality was just what she needed to jolt some sense into her. She picked up the hammer again but before she could start swinging it a light tap at the door alerted her to Liam's arrival.

"Still need a hand or did my big mouth make you mad enough to give you superhero powers?" He looked at her sheepishly as he pushed the door wide open.

Georgie ignored his attempt at humour and pointed to the corner, where the piece of wood was propped against the wall. "That's the one I need help to lift."

Liam walked over to the wall and she indicated the supports up near the ceiling. "I'll need to get up on the ladder to get one end up there, if you can just take the weight at the other end?"

Much to her relief, he'd put a T-shirt on before he'd come up, and he hefted the piece of wood up to his chest while she dragged the small stepladder across the room. "I'm not used to working by myself. I'm sorry I had to—" She cut herself off as he looked at her. Climbing the first two rungs of the ladder brought her just above the top of his head and she looked down at him. "Okay." She put her hands up. "No more apologies. Cross my heart." She climbed up another rung and reached down for the lumber. "Ready?"

Liam lifted it up to her and Georgie gripped the wood firmly before she positioned it into the support in the corner.

"Keep a hold on your end, please. I just need to move the ladder over a bit more." She climbed down and because Liam was holding the wood in place, she had to duck beneath his arm to pull the small ladder across to reach the other support. She ignored the jolt as his arm brushed against her shoulder and she quickly climbed back up the stepladder and reached out for the wood. Her hands grasped the end and she slotted it into place.

Georgie leaned back to survey the wall, conscious of Liam's proximity. She forgot she was on the top step of the small ladder and stepped into mid-air. She let out a gasp as her arms flailed for a second. With a nimble turn, she twisted and jumped onto the floor, her heavy boots just missing Liam's bare feet. Unfortunately for Georgie, she teetered forward as she landed, coming up hard against his chest. His arms went around her and her head banged against his shoulder.

"Oomph." Closing her eyes, she stood there for a moment catching her breath. Finally, she lifted her head and looked up at him. "Sorry," she whispered.

"Are you okay?" Liam's voice was husky, and a shiver spiralled down her spine. Georgie stiffened in his arms so that he wouldn't feel the effect he was having on her body. She had turned to mush, not to mention that her resolve to remain unaffected by him had gone flying out the window. Her heart was thudding and as she looked up at him, she could see a pulse flickering in his cheek.

Why is he looking at me like that? His eyes were fixed on hers, and he had the strangest expression on his face. Georgie tried to pull back, but he tightened his hold around her. Chest to chest and thigh to thigh, she felt the tremble that rippled through him. She stopped pulling away as another exquisite shiver ran down her back.

"Do you mind if I just hold you?" His words were soft and his voice ragged, as though he'd been the one exerting himself. "It's been a long time since

I've held anyone this close."

Georgie looked back at him and when she saw her own need reflected in his eyes, her arms lifted, almost of their own accord. She stood on her toes, reached around his neck, linking her fingers beneath his long hair, and lifted her face to rest against his cheek.

His face was cool against her heated skin. Liam's lips gently slid across her cheek in a soft kiss that was full of yearning. He paused before his lips reached hers. It was like coming home; different from any other kiss she'd ever experienced before. After a moment, he moved his head back a little before he rested his cheek against hers again. His lashes brushed her skin as soft as a butterfly and the rasp of his unshaven chin rubbed against her cheek. They stood locked together, no words, no movement, and Georgie revelled in the comfort of his closeness.

Finally, Liam pulled away and she frowned as the cool air replaced the warmth of his skin against hers. She looked up and he was staring into the distance above her head, and she looked down knowing she wasn't going to like what he was about to say.

She put her hand up before he could speak. "That was very sweet but it was a mistake and we both know it."

He lowered his head and stared at her for a

moment before shoving his hands in his pockets.

"Yeah, it was. I'm sorry."

Georgie's phone trilled in her pocket as Liam turned on his heel and left her alone.

Chapter Eight

"Would it be okay with you if Jack drops me off on the way to Brisbane?" Sienna launched straight into her conversation as Georgie tried to compose herself. She gripped the phone tightly against her ear and tried to concentrate on what Sienna was saying.

"Yes…that's fine…no problem. Are you still coming tonight?" She lifted her hand and touched her cheek, trying to hold on to the feeling of Liam's lips on her skin.

"Yes, we're about to leave Noosa now. We realised it was crazy for me to go all the way to Brisbane and come back down to Hideaway Bay, so Jack's going to leave the car at the airport. Are you at home now?"

"No." Loose tendrils of Georgie's hair had come adrift from her ponytail. She lifted her hand from her cheek to push it back from her face and was surprised to see her fingers trembling. What had passed between her and Liam in those few minutes had rocked her to the core. When he had stepped back from her and let her go, it was like being cast adrift. It was a feeling she had never experienced before. She was aware of her heart thudding, and she drew in a deep breath trying to stop the lightness in her chest. "But I'm almost done here. I'll head home soon."

"Can't wait to see you."

"You, too. Bye." Georgie disconnected the call and slipped the phone back into her pocket. Now she had an excuse to leave and go home. She needed to escape from the house before she went looking for Liam to take up where they'd left off, even though she knew that was the last thing she should do.

Taking a final look, Georgie scanned the room, making sure all the electrical tools were switched off and unplugged before she closed the window. She didn't want to start a fire in this beautiful old house. As well as needing a restoration, she was sure the wiring wasn't up to code. The whole house needed work, and her fingers itched to be a part of bringing it back to life.

The afternoon sun was streaming through the window, bathing the half-built shelves in the strong light reflected by the large expanse of glass in the walls. Liam would have to put some sort of window covering up before he filled the shelves, or his books would fade quickly. Maybe he'd need Mitzi's frilly curtains, after all. The glimmer of a smile tugged at her lips, and Georgie knew she needed to lighten up. As she packed up her tools, she looked around, imagining what a beautiful room this would be once the shelves were finished and lined with books. Polished floorboards covered with a rich traditional rug, a desk sitting beneath the window… She shook her head and focused on tidying up. Not her house, and she wouldn't be here to see it finished, anyway. Closing the door behind her, she focused on the night ahead with Sienna.

Mutt looked at her mournfully as she pushed opened the gate to Ana's cottage. There'd been no sign of Liam when she'd let herself out of his house. Tomorrow, Sienna would be working with her, and hopefully that would put the end to any more almost-kisses from Liam. Georgie grabbed Mutt's lead and whistled for him. A walk on the beach would clear her head.

The walk on the firm wet sand at the edge of the small waves did do her a power of good, despite getting soaked from Mutt frolicking in the shallow water. She threw driftwood for him and he chased it and dropped it at her feet. He made the walk more enjoyable. She'd have to get herself a dog.

Shoot. She couldn't. Why did she keep forgetting she was going overseas? How could she forget about the around-the-world trip looming ahead of her? She had plenty of money in the bank and an amazing adventure planned. What was the big deal about leaving home?

She was almost thirty, for goodness' sake.

Leaving for Hawaii on Christmas Eve? First

stop at a luxurious beachfront house on Niu Beach, ten miles out of Honolulu. Most people would give anything to be in the position she was. Why, then, was she less than enthusiastic? Wandering upstairs, Georgie pulled off her T-shirt and turned on the taps of the deep bath in the small bathroom. Once she sat down with Sienna and a glass of wine, she'd get some excitement happening about this trip. Maybe Sienna could meet her in Machu Picchu for their birthday like they'd talked about at their last birthday dinner. She needed to cheer herself up and stop mulling over what couldn't be changed. Whatever had happened in the past had to stay there and now she must move on.

Life goes on, no matter what is thrown at me. She had her health, great friends and family, a job that would be there when she came back from her trip, and enough money to have a good life, if she was careful. She'd gotten over the need to have a significant other in her life.

So why do I feel so unsettled? Liam's face flashed into her thoughts. She'd known the man less than a week, and it was time to push this unwelcome attraction aside.

Ana's bathroom was filled with an array of bath oils, soaps, and salts. Georgie chose a bottle of amber and musk salts, and let the powder trickle between her fingers into the steaming water, taking a deep breath as the Oriental fragrance filled the small room. She slipped her shorts and panties off and stepped into the water, sighing as the heat warmed her chilled skin. She lay in there for half an hour, deliberately pushing Liam from her mind, despite the number of times his sexy eyes filled her thoughts.

Ice-blue eyes that stayed with you, filled with sadness and secrets.

We are a fine pair.

The water cooled and she climbed out of the bath and picked up one of the fluffy pink towels from the shelf beneath the window. Ana had an eye for pretty things and this bathroom was a lovely room. When she bought her own place—when she came home from overseas—she'd do something similar in her own bathroom. Georgie hummed and grinned to herself as she wrapped the soft towel around her.

But without the pink. Definitely without the pink. The tune from *Pretty in Pink* filled her mind and she hummed as she patted herself dry.

She didn't hear the car come up the drive but a soft tap at the front door heralded Sienna's arrival. Georgie twisted her wet hair into a knot on the top of her head and knotted the towel above her breasts before she ran lightly down the stairs. The carpet was soft and deep beneath her bare feet. It was a relief to have her heavy work boots off.

"You're early!" She pulled open the door and

gasped as Liam's face filled her vision. Not in her thoughts this time, but standing in the doorway with his mouth hanging open and his eyes wide with appreciation

***

Liam couldn't help himself. All thoughts of spare parts and welcome parties fled from his mind as the door was flung open. He'd come down to see Georgie to get the old dears' number so he could take a rain check on the welcome party on Sunday. He'd totally forgotten about the invitation. He'd been out in the garage when he'd come across some Fireflite parts, and he remembered he was supposed to be going there on Sunday. The parts he'd found certainly weren't pink, but they were indeed Fireflite spares. He'd had a bit of a chuckle and put them aside in a small box. The old girls had been telling the truth. Now the box was tucked beneath his arm as he rapped on Georgie's door.

He'd done his best to put Georgie out of his mind since he'd held and almost kissed her, even though he knew he was kidding himself. Cancelling Sunday was an excuse. He'd wanted to see Georgie again. When she'd left early, he'd resisted the urge to come out of his study in case she'd thought he was having a go at her about her hours again.

"You're early!" The words were followed by a gasp as a prettily wrapped parcel of pure woman, encased in a pink towel, stared at him. Liam dropped his eyes to the bare legs at the bottom of the towel and then lifted his gaze to the hands that were covering the knotted towel above her breasts. A heavy musky fragrance enveloped him and he closed his mouth. He was gaping like an adolescent.

"Liam! What are you doing here?" Georgie's face was flushed and tendrils of wet hair stuck to her neck and cheeks. "I thought you were my sis…my cousin."

Her eyes were wide as she raised her hand to push back the wet hair, and the towel slipped a fraction lower. Liam didn't fight the grin he knew was spreading over his face. He'd been uncomfortable about facing Georgie after their "hug," but now he was pleased he'd chosen this particular time to come and see her. The ice was broken. Well and truly—in shards.

"Stop looking at me like that." Her voice was stern. Her green eyes fairly glowed.

"Like what?" he asked innocently, doing exactly what she asked him not to do. Hell, she made too pretty a picture to look away.

"You know what." She slipped him a tentative smile and his eyes fixed on her lips as she half closed the door to block his view, and peered around it. He'd never noticed the full curve of her bottom lip before; she'd usually been concentrating on banging a piece of wood or sticking a bandage on his head or dealing with two recalcitrant old ladies. Come to think of it, he'd never seen her standing so still before, apart from when he'd kissed her this afternoon. She was always moving around doing something.

"Wait there. I'll be back in five minutes. Don't go away." Her irritation with him was now mixed with faint amusement at the look he knew was on his face. If it was anything like he was feeling, he must look like a stupefied adolescent with his mouth hanging open in a silly grin.

She was beautiful. *Drop. Dead. Gorgeous.*

Even in her work clothes and heavy boots with her hair pulled back from her face, she'd made a lasting impression on him. But now wrapped in that pink towel, all flushed and rosy with tendrils of wet hair trailing down her shoulders and stuck to that alabaster white skin…well…she was bewitching. Words failed Liam. His mouth dried at the thought of running his hands over her soft curves.

But it was way past time to gather himself together and stop acting like a fool. He put the box on the floor next to the door and walked along the porch. There was an old cane chair near the steps and he flopped down into it, and leaned his head back against the wall. A cat lying along the table beside the chair lifted its head and opened one eye before deciding he wasn't worth the effort of moving. It stretched and then curled itself back up into a ball.

Liam refused to let himself think. But he had to. His brain was going in the direction his body was telling it to. The sooner he told Georgie why he was here and hightail it back up the hill, the better for all concerned. He knew she was aware of the spark between them, but he wasn't ready to do anything about it.

He'd never be ready for it.

Not with her.

For a fling or a one-night stand, okay, he might be interested. But Georgie was a neighbour, and too close to his new home to get involved with on a casual basis. If he was going to settle into his new house and this community, she was the last person he'd choose to get involved with.

Not because he didn't want her but despite her confidence, there was an air of fragility about her. In spite of her heavy boots, and her skill with a hammer and nails, he knew she was vulnerable beneath the tough exterior she presented to the world, and he could tell she'd been hurt badly somewhere along the line. And the last thing he wanted was another needy woman in his life.

Whoever the guy was, he had obviously been a fool. The few moments this afternoon when Georgie had clung to him before he'd pulled back had been pure heaven. Liam had to fight the temptation to go there again. Her pale skin and her green eyes had stayed in his mind. He hadn't noticed the deep green depths of them until they'd widened when she had opened the door.

Man, he had it bad. He looked across at the door, tempted to just leave the parts on the porch and head home before she came out. But he couldn't leave; he had to tell Georgie he wasn't going to make the welcome party at Thelma and Mitzi's.

As he looked along the porch toward his escape route up the hill, a little red sports car turned off the highway and slowed to a stop on the grass just inside the gate.

Great, now she's got visitors. It must be her cousin she was expecting. Liam pushed himself to his feet and watched as a tall, solid man climbed out of the driver's side. A pang of jealousy hit Liam in the gut. He was a fool. It looked like Georgie already had a boyfriend. His overactive imagination had kicked in, and he'd dreamed up a sad past for her. That same imagination had sucked him into dreaming up a future with Vanessa, and fool that he still was, he'd been about to go down the same path with Georgie. Okay, maybe not planning a future, but he'd been more attracted to her than he should have been. From now on, he'd use his imagination for his stories.

Liam headed for the steps, ready to leave, but paused when the guy went around and opened the passenger door. A petite woman with black hair cut in a bob climbed out and looked over at the house before she linked her arm through the guy's. They walked over to the steps together.

"Hi, I'm Sienna." The tiny woman let go of the man's arm and several gold bangles jangled on her arm as she held her hand out to him. "And this is Jack. You must be Liam?"

He took her hand briefly before nodding at her and then shaking the hand of the tall guy standing beside her. "Yes, that's right. I'm Liam from up the hill. Pleased to meet you both."

"Georgie told us you were living next door. How do you like living in Joe's old place?" Jack shook his hand firmly while Sienna stared up at him. Her eyes were circled by dark black pencil, and her skin was as fair as Georgie's.

"I haven't been here long, but it seems like a nice quiet place, so far. Great house."

"I won't pretend we don't know who you are, but you probably do get sick of people telling you they love your books?" Sienna crossed her arms and smiled at him.

Liam laughed. She was brash and up-front, and he liked the vibes he was getting from her. "No, an author never gets sick of hearing that. If we didn't want to please our readers, there'd be no point writing the stories in the first place."

"Good. Well, I can tell you I loved them all. Hey, Sooky." She reached down and patted the cat as it wound around her legs before switching a curious gaze back to him. "Is Georgie home?"

"Er, yes. She's just getting dressed. Look, I'll go back to my place and leave you to your visit. I can see her later."

"No, please don't leave on our account." Jack slung his arm around Sienna's shoulder. "I'm only here for a minute to say hello to Georgie before I head off to the airport. I'm catching the late flight to Melbourne."

"Yes, please stay. I'd love to chat with you some more." Sienna grinned wickedly. "I know Georgie wouldn't have talked to you about your books. She'd never heard of you."

"I know. I imagine she's too busy working to read. She's always on the go."

"You've got her number and you've only known her a few days." Sienna shot him an intent look. "Yes, our Georgie has kept herself very busy lately. That's one of the reasons I've come to visit," she added enigmatically.

Liam sensed there was more behind her words, but before he could comment, the door opened. Georgie stepped out and her face lit up in a sweet smile.

"You're here." She hurried over to greet the couple.

Liam's heart took off. She wore a floaty pale green dress, and she'd dried her hair and left it loose in a cloud around her face. A touch of pale pink lipstick highlighted her lips and the same sweet fragrance reached him as she moved past him to Sienna. As the light caught her from behind, the curves of her body were silhouetted through the thin fabric. Every sensible thought disappeared from his mind.

"Hey, sis." The two women shared a warm hug before Georgie turned to Jack with a broad smile. "How's my favourite sculptor?"

Jack leaned down and kissed Georgie's cheek as he took her hand. "You're looking particularly gorgeous this afternoon." Another shaft of jealousy lodged in Liam's chest.

Georgie coloured bright red and put her hands to her cheeks. "Thank you. I figured if we were having a girls' night, I might as well dress like a girl."

Liam watched without speaking as Sienna narrowed her eyes and then looked back at him. "Very dolled up for a night at home, Georgie." Her voice was droll.

If it was possible, Georgie's cheeks flushed even more as she waved a hand at Sienna. "I've been in work clothes and boots all week. I felt like a change."

Liam let his gaze follow her hands, and then kept going down to her feet. He was used to seeing her in heavy work boots, but now her feet were bare, and her toenails were painted a soft shell pink. He could tell she was uncomfortable, and he decided to make himself scarce. Although he would have preferred to stay here on the porch drinking in the sight of her for a little while longer. His arms itched to reach out and pull her close, even with the two people who were watching him with interest. Sienna's stare was particularly sharp—and protective, if he was reading her right.

"I've left a box of car parts by the door." He held Georgie's gaze as he schooled his expression into a casual look.

"Car parts?" She cocked her head to the side and her brow wrinkled in a frown.

"Yes, parts for an old Fireflite, but they're not pink." He grinned at her as she realised what he was talking about. She burst out laughing and put her hands over her mouth.

"Are you telling me those two naughty women were actually telling the truth?" She held his eyes steadily.

"Seems like they were."

"Don't tell me…Mitzi and Thelma?" Sienna

looked from one to the other with a grin before she settled her gaze on Liam. "I've already had the call and been invited to your welcome reception. You do know half the town is coming to meet you on Sunday? I hope you're ready for the old folk of Maleny."

"I hope you didn't come up here especially for that, did you?" he asked. Damn, maybe it was too late to get out of it.

Sienna shook her head. "I'm here to help Georgie, but I did say I'd love to come. I wouldn't miss one of Thelma and Mitzi's dos."

Liam turned to Georgie. "That's why I came over to your place, apart from dropping in the spare parts. I was going to cancel on Sunday but I didn't know how to get in touch with them.

Georgie shook her head. "That would be a real shame. They'll be so disappointed. Do you have something else going on?"

Liam shook his head slowly and tried to focus. He was having trouble taking his eyes off Georgie's pretty mouth. "Not really, just a writing deadline. I have to go to Brisbane on Tuesday and I must get some chapters done before I go." He stared across the top of the porch railing out to the ocean. "I've been a bit preoccupied and I'm way behind with this book."

"It's up to you." Georgie put her hand out and

touched his hand and the zing went skittering all the way to his shoulder. "They can still have a party…they often have a Sunday get-together—"

He cut her off before she could finish. "No, it's too short notice. It would be rude. I should have cancelled it earlier. Are you still okay to give me a ride? I don't have a car yet."

"I guess so. Now that Sienna's here to help me, we'll get a lot more done on your bookshelves tomorrow than I would have by myself."

Liam was surprised and turned to Sienna. "You've come down to help with the job at my place?"

Sienna shot him a lazy grin. "Yep, you get a double dose of Sacchi tomorrow."

He looked from one to the other. "So you're sisters?"

"We were for twenty-nine years. In fact, we were twins."

He looked from to the other in confusion and caught Georgie frowning at Sienna. "Were?"

"It's a long story, but we don't have time for it now." Sienna glanced down at her watch. "And it's time for you to hit the road, Jack."

Jack shook Liam's hand. "I'll look forward to catching up with you on Sunday, Liam."

He hugged Georgie and looped his arm around Sienna's shoulder. "Come on, woman. Give me a fitting farewell."

Liam stood next to Georgie as the couple walked back toward the sports car. Sienna looked up at Jack and the love in her face hit Liam in the gut. No one had ever looked at him like that, not even his wife. He glanced across at Georgie. She was blinking away a tear.

"They look good together, don't they?" She sniffed and smiled at him. "They've only been together a few months. And they're so happy."

"Do they live close by?" He was curious about Georgie's background.

"No, down the coast in Lake Weyba. Sienna bought one of the houses we restored." She looked at him and Liam's stomach did a double flip as he tried to keep his eyes off her lips. The glossy pink stuff on them glistened in the afternoon light. "We used to be in business together but now Sienna and Jack have an art gallery in Noosa…and Ana has gone to Melbourne with her partner, Blake, for a while."

They stood side by side on the porch and watched as Jack lifted Sienna onto the hood of the car and stood in front of her with his hands on her shoulders. She grabbed the back of his head and pulled his face to her with a joyful laugh.

Liam turned to Georgie, as the moment between Jack and Sienna was a private one for lovers and he felt uncomfortable intruding on it. "I'll head on home now. I guess I'll see you both tomorrow?"

"If you're not busy. We'll probably come over early." She looked up at him with a smile. "I'd like to make the most of Sienna being here. Your bookshelves will truly be unique once she puts her touch on them."

Liam felt like a teenage boy on his first date. He knew he should go but he was finding it hard to leave. The thought of returning to the empty house up the hill was unappealing, especially when Georgie was standing here with a welcoming smile.

A smile directed solely at him. A smile wide enough to make his toes curl.

"Don't go yet. Sienna will be really upset if she doesn't get to talk to you. She's probably brought a load of her books with her for you to sign." The expression on Georgie's face weakened his resolve. She wanted him to stay, too, and then she confirmed it. "In fact, why don't you stay for dinner? I can give you our neighbourly welcome."

She looked horrified as soon as the words left her lips. Those shiny, kissable lips.

He intended to decline but he accepted before his brain kicked into gear. "Sure. I'd love to." What the heck was wrong with his mouth? It was apparently disconnected from his brain.

Sienna and Jack were still in a clinch by the car, and Liam shot them a glance before turning back to Georgie. "I'll go back up the hill and get some wine after Jack leaves." He didn't want to intrude on their privacy even if it was in the middle of the driveway.

"No, come on in. We don't need anything. Jack and Sienna will be ages yet." Her embarrassment had disappeared and she smoothed her hand down the skirt of her floaty dress. His whole body began to buzz with arousal, and the need to put his arms around her and hold her close took over once more.

Thank goodness Mutt chose that very moment to come bounding around the side of the porch and careered to a stop beside them, dropping a wet slobbery ball onto Georgie's bare feet.

"Eww, Mutt! I wondered where you'd gotten to." She reached down and rubbed her hands through his damp fur. "You're wet! You've been down on the beach haven't you, you naughty dog?"

Liam managed to push away the feelings that threatened to take control of him as the dog pushed between them. Maybe staying here any longer was not such a good idea.

"He gets out through a gap in the fence. I'll have to fix it...or leave him inside for the night." Georgie frowned. "I worry about him going in the water. He loves it."

"Yeah, and you've already done one rescue

down on the beach this week."

She gave him a little smile. "Don't remind me. That was embarrassing. I thought you'd drowned and you didn't need any help at all."

Liam lowered his voice and reached out and took her hand. "I'm sorry for being rude to you that afternoon. I was in such a cranky mood…and I was embarrassed that I'd fallen out of the kayak." He let a smile play about his lips. "If I'm honest, I was a bit sorry you didn't try mouth-to-mouth on me."

Georgie coloured brick red and laughed. "I was going through the first aid steps in my mind when I first saw you lying there."

He looked down. Her hand was still in his. Even though her fingernails were short and he could feel a slight callus on one palm, her nails were painted the same soft pink as her toenails. She worked so hard, and it was good to see her relaxed and joking with him.

"How about I give you a hand to fix the fence? Not that I'm much good with tools and things."

The memory of helping her today when she'd fallen off the ladder came flooding back, and Liam let go of her hand, trying to focus his attention on something other than Georgie. The throaty roar of the car saved him, and he reached down to retrieve the ball from beside her feet. He was getting way too sucked in here by a beautiful barefoot woman in a pretty dress.

"I'll have a look at the fence while Sienna decides what's for dinner. Have you seen the orchard behind the house yet?" Georgie picked up a towel and began to wipe the dog down as Sienna walked up the steps.

Sienna leaned against the steps. "I'm doing dinner?"

Georgie caught his eye and despite his brain telling him to pull back, his insides swirled as her lips parted in a huge smile. She'd smiled more in fifteen minutes than he'd seen in a week and it was doing his head—and the rest of his body—in.

"Yep, it was a girls' night in, I told you that."

"Was?" Sienna tipped her head to the side.

"I've invited Liam to stay, so now it's a dinner party." Liam was fascinated by the unfamiliar teasing tone in Georgie's voice.

The swirling dress, the loose hair, and the smile on her face turned her into one altogether tempting package.

"So what are we eating, Sienna?" Georgie asked innocently.

A look that could lure a man to his doom. *Ugh, maybe I should write poetry instead.*

Chapter Nine

Georgie's heart was doing crazy things. When she looked at Liam it was almost skipping a beat. And when his sexy blue eyes held hers, it beat so hard it thudded in her chest. She didn't have a clue what had possessed her to invite him to stay for dinner, and she was already regretting the invitation. An independent woman would know better than to get involved with her next-door neighbour. But try telling that to her nerve endings. They were skittering all over the place. Logic said *no*, this was not the way to independence. Her body said *yes,* go for it. Georgie wanted him to be here, and close to her, even with Sienna there. It was the strangest feeling.

Georgie had tried to cover her confusion by teasing Sienna about cooking dinner. Her pantry was well stocked. She'd driven into Maleny earlier and had plenty of food, but Sienna always bit back when she was teased.

She was also looking at Georgie and Liam now with a speculative gleam in her eye. "Well, in that case, it's just as well I got a huge order of Indian takeout on the way over. Raj is delivering it at seven o'clock." Sienna grinned at Liam. "Neither of us cooks very well. It certainly doesn't reflect our Italian upbringing."

Sienna held Georgie's eye and there was a

question on her face. Georgie knew she was going to get the third degree when they were alone later, but her relationship with Liam was as a neighbour and a client only, and she would make that quite clear to her cousin. Despite these unfamiliar feelings surging through her, she was only being neighbourly. It had nothing to do with feeling sorry for him being alone, or that she couldn't get the feel of his mouth against her cheek out of her thoughts. She turned to Sienna. "Mutt got out again. Do you want to come for a walk? Liam's going to help me fix the fence."

"No. I'll unpack and maybe read a bit by the window." Sienna waved a lazy hand and turned to Liam. "I know Georgie's going to work me to death tomorrow, so I need to rest up."

Mutt ran ahead of Georgie and Liam as they walked through the backyard. They walked close together, side by side, almost touching, but not quite. Liam chuckled as the dog ran past the gate that opened into the orchard and pushed his nose against a loose piece of fencing. The plank lifted and with a happy *woof* he ran into the orchard and onto the path that led down to the beach.

"There's the escape hole." Liam pointed to the hole in the fence. "It doesn't look big enough for him to get through, though.

"He's determined. I know Ana's had a lot of trouble keeping him in. He adores the water. Mutt!

Come back here." Georgie pushed open the gate and stepped into the orchard as the dog ignored her call. "Mutt. Now!" She hadn't stopped to slip on her shoes, and the grass was cold and damp beneath her bare feet as the afternoon drew to a close and the sea mist settled onto the ground.

The large dog slowed down, turned, and slunk back to them with his tail between his legs.

"He loves to run on the beach and I haven't had a chance to take him down there much this week." Georgie drew in a deep breath. Small buds were beginning to form on the trees despite some of them still being loaded with ripe oranges. A couple of late blooms lingered and a whiff of sweet fragrance drifted on the late-afternoon breeze.

"I love this house. One day I'd like to live along the water and have my own place that looks out to the sea." She was babbling, but there was tension hanging in the air between them and she willed it to go away.

Liam walked over to the fence and turned around to stare at her. Her feet seemed to be stuck to the ground and she dropped her gaze, while trying to stop her legs from trembling. Mutt walked along beside her and she curled her fingers in his soft fur.

"Your perfume smells like the orange blossoms," Liam said quietly as she reached him. Being close to him made her heartbeat pick up again and Georgie swallowed, trying to ground herself. She was in trouble here. No matter how much she told herself she wasn't going to fall for her sexy neighbour, her insides were like jelly as his soft words washed over her. Inviting Liam to stay for dinner had been foolish. Bringing him out into the orchard, doubly so. She should have just taken the car part or whatever was in the box he'd left on the porch and let him go home. She had to stay away from him and spend as little time in his company as she could, despite the job. This trembling feeling and uncertainty, the wanting to be with him, were new to her; she'd never experienced them with any guy before, even when they'd gotten to the sleeping-with-each-other stage. Sure, she'd enjoyed their company and she'd had a few relationships that had lasted for a while, but this all-encompassing wanting-to-be-next-to-him feeling was throwing her for a loop.

It must be his good looks and fame. That's all it was.

"It's my shampoo," she said, and as she spoke the wind picked up her hair and whipped it across her eyes. Liam lifted one hand and brushed her hair gently away from her face.

"I like your hair down." He stared at her with those sexy blue eyes. Each of his dark lashes was clearly outlined and the pupils in the centre of his eyes were dark. It wasn't fair that a man could have such beautiful eyes. Georgie couldn't look away. His hand was still on her face and as she stared back at him, he slid it gently back through the loose curls, and placed his fingers on the back of her neck. "You look really different without it pulled back off your face."

Georgie swallowed and attempted some self-deprecating humour. "Yeah, the red is more obvious when it's out and loose."

"It's not red. It's a beautiful golden copper." Liam still hadn't taken his eyes from hers. His intent stare was turning her insides to mush.

"Well, I suppose being an author, you can always find the nicer words." She stepped away from his hold, willing her heart to settle, and gave herself a little internal shake.

For some reason he's flirting with me. "It's red to me. I've put up with plenty of teasing because of it." Georgie kept her voice matter-of-fact.

She was reading way too much into the way he was looking at her and the way his fingers were gently caressing the back of her neck. But when Liam put out his other hand, took her arm, and pulled her against him again, she knew she wasn't imagining the intent in his expression. She stared back at him as he moved both hands to cradle her face. He held her gaze as he lowered his head and she lifted her face just like she had the other day. She couldn't help herself, any more than she could stop her heart from thumping madly. Their lips met and clung, sweetly and gently, and as he increased the warm pressure, a shiver ran right down to her toes. She leaned into him and Liam moved one hand to the back of her head to hold her close.

Not that she wanted to move away. Georgie lifted her hand to his face and brushed her fingers against the rough stubble on his cheeks. It felt as sexy as it looked, and she let out a contented, soft sigh against his lips. Closing her eyes, she opened her mouth to him as he deepened the kiss and let his tongue slide over her bottom lip. Georgie didn't know how long they stood there in the late-afternoon sunshine with the breeze blowing her hair around them. It was how she'd always dreamed a kiss should be. The physical sensations, the emotion filling her, and the euphoria of being held so gently in Liam's arms as his lips explored hers left her stunned. She couldn't gather her thoughts together while she was in this dreamlike state, but she knew they shouldn't be doing this.

When Mutt finally pushed his wet nose between them and whimpered, Georgie opened her eyes and pulled her head back slowly. She swallowed and closed her eyes, licking her lips nervously as she took a moment to compose herself. Finally, she found her voice and managed to speak firmly…almost.

"We shouldn't be doing this." She dropped her arms to her sides and stepped back, almost falling over Mutt in her anxiety to put some distance between her and Liam.

"Probably not." Liam didn't move away as she expected. "But I couldn't help myself."

"Let's get this fence fixed." Her voice was husky but steady.

Georgie turned away to the fence, trying to shove her trembling hands in her pockets before she realised she was wearing a dress and not her usual work shorts with their deep pockets. Nervously, she clenched her hands in front of her until they steadied.

"There's a piece of wood beneath the middle row of the oranges trees." She pointed across the orchard. "If you can get it for me, we can leverage it to stop this loose piece of fence. Mutt won't be able to get out again if we wedge something against the bottom." She was desperately trying to return to normality. Her heart was beating so fast she was sure she would fall into a dead faint or a swoon at his feet if it didn't settle. Taking a deep breath, she closed her eyes for a moment and focused on breathing in and out.

By the time Liam had dragged the large slab of old wood across to the fence, Georgie almost had herself under control. Physically anyway, but all the fears that had been plaguing her about falling for the next man who came along had resurfaced.

I'm overreacting. It was a simple kiss between a man and a woman in a romantic setting. Don't read too much into it.

Treat it lightly and don't act like a love-struck fool. But when she was done talking to herself, she brushed her fingers across her lips to capture the remnants of the kiss that lingered.

"Here you go." Liam let go of the slab of wood and frowned, concentrating on the loose plank in the fence. Georgie dropped her hand away from her mouth.

"Which side do you think would be best?" he asked.

Georgie was pleased to have something concrete to focus on, and she walked through the gate and looked at the fence from both sides. "Definitely the outside. I'll hold this down while you shove it underneath."

Liam crouched down beside her, wedged the wood beneath the plank, and gave a satisfied grunt when it held. "Now all you need is a small rock to fill in the hole where he's been digging and it should be blocked."

Georgie looked around the garden. There was a small pile of rocks in the garden by the children's play equipment. "Over there." They were both apparently going to pretend that the kiss hadn't happened. Liam followed her over and she bent to pick up the rock.

"That's too heavy. Let me help you." He stepped past her.

The piece of rock was long and narrow and as he reached to take one end, his fingers brushed against hers and Georgie almost dropped it. She lowered her eyes as they lifted it together, and they walked sideways across the garden and through the gate. Georgie concentrated on watching where she was walking so she didn't have to make eye contact with Liam. They manoeuvred the piece of stone near the hole at the bottom of the loose plank and as she bent to secure her end, Liam's shadow fell across her. His jeans-clad thigh brushed against her leg and she jumped as a hot jolt ran down to her toes. She stumbled and the rock slipped from her grasp and narrowly missed her bare feet. Luckily, it landed in the space it was meant for and she let out a sigh of relief.

"That was close. Sorry I let go too soon." Even to her ears, her voice was breathless, and she risked a glance up at him through her lashes. She couldn't remember ever wanting anyone to hold her the way she wanted Liam to hold her. No one had ever had this effect on her. Just as well; it was wreaking havoc with her breathing and her composure.

He didn't move. "I think I'd better pass on the dinner invite. If I'm going to spend Sunday away from my desk, I really should get back to my writing tonight."

"That's probably a good idea. I'm sorry I've taken up so much of your afternoon." She bit her lip as she realised she was apologising again.

"Saying sorry again?" Liam lifted his hand and brushed his knuckles across her cheek as the heat rushed up her neck to her face. "You sure get a great blush going."

"Sorry, it's my fair skin." She shrugged with a little laugh. "Oh, you know what I mean." His fingers lingered on her face and Georgie closed her eyes fighting the urge to lift her hand and hold Liam's fingers against her cheek. He was standing so close she could drop her head onto his shoulder and lean on him.

"Oh, what the heck." Liam's other arm came around her and he pulled her close. "I was going to leave because I knew if I didn't I'd kiss you again."

Her head flew up and warmth rushed through her. The afternoon light had faded while they'd worked, and his face was shadowed, making the angles of his face sharper. But his eyes were soft and his mouth…she let her gaze linger on the lips that had given her so much pleasure just a little while ago.

Nervously she flicked her tongue out over her lips and Liam groaned.

Georgie closed her eyes and reached her arms up around his neck. She forced away all of the reasons why she shouldn't be kissing him and lost herself in his kiss. She hoped Sienna wasn't sitting at the window.

That's all I need.

Chapter Ten

Liam had reluctantly headed up the hill after he'd kissed her senseless and Georgie knew she had a smile on her face when he waved to her.

"I'll see you tomorrow," he called back as he went through the gate. "Tell Sienna I'll catch up with her then."

Georgie pushed open the door to the house. Her legs were still trembling and her bare feet felt as though they were walking on air. Sienna was leaning back in the chair, by the window—*of course*—waiting for her to come in.

"Where's lover boy gone?" Sienna grinned at her. "Wow, Georgie. You've sure moved fast this time. And what a honey! He, my dear, is drop-dead gorgeous."

"I haven't moved at all," Georgie snapped. "And there's nothing going on."

Sienna tapped a finger against her lips. "There was from where I was watching. You know if I hadn't been here, I'm pretty sure the two of you would be heading for your bedroom about now."

Georgie shrugged, trying to stay nonchalant. "Maybe." The thought of having Liam in her bedroom sent the fire racing to her cheeks and she lifted her hands to her face. Her self-control slipped and she finally shook her head and dropped onto the sofa next to Sienna's chair.

"It was a silly thing to do."

"Why? Didn't look too silly to me; in fact, it looked pretty good from here." Sienna's eyes were dancing. "You're a dark horse. How long's this been going on? He's only just moved in, hasn't he?"

"There's nothing happening. I fell off the ladder the other day and we had a bit of a…moment and then that…that kiss just came from nowhere and it…it…blew my socks off." She leaned back and covered her eyes. "Holy hell, I can't stop shaking."

Sienna burst out laughing. "You should see the look on your face. I've never seen you look like that. *Ever*."

Georgie put her fingers on her mouth. The problem was she shouldn't have let the kiss affect her like that, and she shouldn't have kissed him back. "But it's not going anywhere."

"Why? He seems like a really nice guy and he's obviously got the hots for you." Sienna tipped her head to the side with a frown. "There's been something wrong with you for a couple of weeks. I knew you had something on your mind. Is it Liam?"

"No. Yes. Sort of." Georgie jumped to her feet and crossed to the kitchen. "How about wine while we wait for dinner?"

Sienna followed her slowly across the room. "And then you can tell me what's going on inside that head of yours."

Georgie reached into the cupboard and pulled out two wineglasses while Sienna hunted up some crackers and cheese. She poured a glass of wine for each of them and carried it back to the chairs in front of the window overlooking the orchard and the ocean. The sun had dropped below the horizon, and a shaft of pink and golden light shattered the low clouds. She looked down at the fence where they had repaired the hole. Where Liam had taken her ever so gently into his arms and given her the kiss of a lifetime. Sienna had been sitting by the window and had seen them. Georgie's face heated again and she placed the cool glass against her cheek as Sienna wandered over and put the plate of snacks on the small table beside them. Georgie was having a hard time understanding what Liam was thinking and why he'd kissed her like that.

"So spill." Sienna looked at her over the top of her glass. "I want to hear all about it. And then you can tell me what's got you so unsettled, if it's not the sexy author up the hill."

Georgie swallowed. It was time to be honest with herself and with Sienna. *Past time.*

"Okay. There are a few things bugging me." Georgie looked over at Sienna, who narrowed her eyes.

"A few?"

"One. When my mother…when Marietta…dropped the news on us a few weeks ago, it explained a lot of things to me."

"What sort of things?" Sienna's eyes were still fixed firmly on her.

"I've never had much luck in love, apparently because it's in my genes." Georgie swallowed. "I just don't have what it takes to commit to a relationship, no matter how much I think I want it. Look how many partners Marietta had in her life, and I haven't even told you about the fiasco with Brent."

"Oh, that's such a load of rubbish and you know it. And who's Brent?"

Georgie waved her hand. "No matter. He's gone now. How many guys have I gone out with over the past ten years? And what's happened with every one of them? They've taken off before we ever got serious."

"It's not about the relationship. It's about the *man*. Finding the right one. How many of those guys did you really want to get serious with? How many times was it that *you* called it quits?" Sienna put her wineglass down and reached over and took Georgie's hand between hers. "Come on, sis. Be honest here. It might sound clichéd but were any of them really Mr. Right?"

"No." Georgie thought back to all the dates she'd had over the past few years. She'd met some great guys, but not one of them had ever lit a spark within her. "None of them, I suppose."

"You and Ana and I were pretty happy working together with our little business. We were all content with our lives, and then Blake came along and you saw what happened there. *Wham.* Ana was lost." Sienna's lips curved in a smile. "If you'd asked me six months ago whether I believed in love and happily ever after, you know what I would have said, don't you? I would have said that what Blake and Ana have is very rare."

Georgie nodded. Sienna had vowed she would never depend on a man.

"And then Jack came along and I fell hard. He was the man for me. And I've never been so happy." Sienna let go of Georgie's hand and cupped her chin in her hand as she rested her elbow on the table. She stared at Georgie. "How can I convince you that you've been trying too hard to find that happiness? You can't search it out. It will happen when the time…and the man…is right."

Georgie shook her head and grinned. "Where's cynical Sienna gone?" She looked around the room. "There's an imposter in her place. Help me find her!"

"Okay, I'll forgive you for that." Sienna grinned back at her. "So that's one reason why you've been mooning around. What else is wrong?"

Georgie sighed. She'd been feeling a little happier for a moment, but she knew she had to be honest. "This trip I'm taking."

"What about it?"

"I don't know what to do. The thought of going away scares me, and being scared scares me, if that makes sense. I'm so settled and secure here on the coast.'

"It will do you good. You spend way too much time worrying about everyone else and solving their problems. You need to get away and take some time for yourself…for the first time in your life." Sienna leaned back in the chair and waved at the view. "This is a beautiful place, but it will be great for you to get away and spread your wings. Let everyone here take care of themselves for a change."

Sienna was right; Georgie thought of her faux pas the other afternoon when she'd offered to be there for Liam. It obviously hadn't scared him away, even though she'd taken off out of his house like a madwoman. For the life of her, she still couldn't understand why he would want to kiss her. Not that there was anything wrong with the kisses. She put her fingers to her lips again.

"Okay, what else? How much does the gorgeous Liam have to do with how flustered you are?" Sienna's voice interrupted her daydreaming.

"Just a little. I've made a fool of myself in

front of him a couple of times."

"So, is that the end of the world? It sure hasn't scared him away, if that's what you were trying to do. It's obvious that he likes you. A lot. Are you going to sleep with him?"

Georgie choked on the wine she was sipping and Sienna leaned forward.

"Well?"

The noise of a car turning into the driveway saved her from answering Sienna's gleeful question. She jumped up and put her glass on the table as she went to take delivery of their Indian food.

Georgie turned to Sienna before she opened the door.

"Promise me one thing? You'll behave while we're working over at Liam's house tomorrow?"

"Of course I'll behave." The wide-eyed innocence on Sienna's face did nothing to reassure Georgie. Why did Thelma and Mitzi and their matchmaking spring to her mind?

Chapter Eleven

Liam's front door was open the next morning when they arrived at the house up on the hill. George had extracted three promises from Sienna while they'd eaten breakfast. One, okay, she wouldn't tease Georgie about Liam. Two, she wouldn't hound him about his books, and three, yes, she would remember that this was a job for a client and not a social visit.

Despite Sienna's reassurances, Georgie's nerves were jumping. Anticipation at seeing Liam curled through her. She'd been tempted for a while to tell Sienna to sleep in, and come up to the house later so she could see Liam alone. But Sienna had bounded out of bed at first light and by the time Georgie had stumbled out of her own bedroom, Sienna was dressed in her work clothes and had their coffee brewing.

"Have you seen my boots, sis?" Sienna was dressed in her work pants but was barefoot.

Despite having spent a restless night, Georgie managed a chuckle and spread her arms innocently. "You've only been here five minutes and you've misplaced your shoes already?"

"Okay, smarty-pants. Where did you hide them?" Sienna punched Georgie lightly on the shoulder as she walked toward the door.

"Me? Do I look like someone who'd steal your shoes?"

Sienna pursed her lips. "The longer it takes me to find them, the longer it will be before we get to lover boy's place."

Georgie grinned and pointed to the door. "You're getting warmer."

"Thank you." Sienna shot her a grin. "It's good to see the old Georgie is still in there somewhere."

Talking to Sienna about her worries had allayed a lot of Georgie's uncertainty, but as the night had gone on, she'd remained firm in her decision that she was not going to get tangled up with Liam. It was only because he was so good-looking and had that vulnerable air about him that she was interested.

Just someone else for me to look after. That's all the appeal was. Nothing else.

Come Tuesday, she would go to Brisbane as she'd planned and organise the rest of her trip. She'd finish the job, stay well out of Liam's way, and remain professional. No more chatting or socialising…or kissing.

She headed through the open door with Sienna close behind, but there was no sign of Liam.

"Shame we didn't get our hands on this place when we were restoring houses." Sienna's voice followed her up the stairs.

"*Ssh*. Liam might be asleep still." Georgie put her fingers to her lips. "He might have stayed up writing till all hours."

Sienna grinned and dropped her voice to a whisper. "Coward. You just don't want him to know we're here."

Georgie glared at her and scurried up the steps, taking care not to tread on the creaking stair. She'd memorised that one the other day. "We may not even see him. Last week, he stayed in his study and I didn't lay eyes on him for days."

Okay, Sienna was right. The warmth pooling in her stomach, the shaking legs, and the increased heartbeat were new to her. Until she got a hold on how she was feeling, and restored her composure, she didn't want to come face-to-face with Liam.

One look at those sexy blue eyes, the shadowed planes of his face, and all her resolve would go out the window. She just knew it. At least Sienna's being here would protect her from any silly behaviour that she was sure to regret.

They worked all morning and Georgie's jangled nerves finally relaxed as they settled into a familiar routine.

"All we need is Ana back here and it would be like old times," Sienna said. Georgie nodded with a smile and went back to marking the lumber for the next cut. She wanted to get as much of the heavy work done while Sienna was here with her today. Then the next time she needed help, she'd call the store and have one of the workers come over to help her lift the shelves into place. Then she wouldn't have to interrupt Liam.

The house was quiet apart from the noise they made hammering and sawing. They were just about to take a break and head back down the hill to Ana's cottage for lunch when the door pushed open.

"Morning." Liam poked his head around the door and Georgie's heart gave a little blip. She dropped the hammer she was holding and went to speak, forgetting she had two nails between her lips.

"M…m…morning." Georgie spat the nails out of her mouth and the usual heat crept up her neck.

Great, red cheeks with a blush staining my skin and he's not even in the room yet.

"I just put a couple of pizzas in the oven. I thought you might like to share lunch with me?" Relief filled Georgie as Liam looked from her to Sienna. She picked the nails up and busied herself with the hammer, willing the colour to leave her face as Sienna answered for them,

"Sounds good to me. I'm starving." She turned to Liam with a smile. "Great timing. We were just about to head down the hill for a break."

Georgie hesitated. "I really need to check on Mutt first. Make sure he hasn't gotten out again."

"I have to go down and get my phone. I'll check on him for you." Sienna winked at her and Georgie frowned. Where had the sister—or rather cousin—gone who didn't believe in love and who'd loathed matchmaking when it had impacted *her* life?

Liam waited while they finished up, and then held the door open as they walked past him into the corridor.

"Thanks, Liam." Sienna followed Georgie toward the steps. Georgie focused on her breathing and tried to keep the heat from her cheeks. She was pleased when Sienna chatted to Liam and kept the conversation going as they walked down to the kitchen. Liam gestured to the table, which was set for three, and they sat down as he pulled some plates from the cupboard.

"I was going to bring my books up for you to sign, but Georgie wouldn't let me."

Liam and Georgie laughed at Sienna as she pouted. Their eyes met and held, and their laughter died away. Georgie pushed her chair back to fill the sudden, awkward silence. "I really need to wash my hands. I've got glue stuck on my fingers."

Sienna's chatter to Liam followed Georgie as she went into the small utility room next to the kitchen. She ran the cold water and patted her cheeks with her wet fingers before she scrubbed her hands. Liam was uncomfortable around her, too. It was obvious. Embarrassment flooded her as she realised he probably regretted kissing her.

Professional and cool. Keep my wits about me and I'll get through this.

She was actually looking forward to getting on that plane and flying to Honolulu on Christmas Eve.

***

Liam tried hard not to look at Georgie as she slipped out to the utility room. Sienna's cool and assessing gaze was fixed firmly on him, and he sensed that beneath the light banter was a mother hen who was looking out for Georgie. He'd spent a restless night trying to figure out what was so fascinating about her, and he regretted kissing her. In the end, he'd gotten out of bed in the early hours and written many new words of the book the publisher was waiting for. The muse had returned in fits and starts. He needed to capture it and hold it.

But he should keep his distance from Georgie. The last thing he needed was to get involved with someone. Someone who would take much-needed focus from his work. He'd come here intending to keep his life private. He hadn't minded being alone before, and there was a big difference between being alone and being lonely. But when he'd been writing in the early hours before dawn, his thoughts had kept going back to a beautiful face surrounded by golden copper-coloured hair, and he could have sworn he could smell that orange blossom fragrance. He'd wondered what it would be like to watch her sleep. Her bottom lip was full and lush, and even when she wasn't smiling he couldn't keep his eyes from her mouth.

At least he'd made a start on the contracted book, and the words were flowing more than they had since he'd come home from Nepal. They were coming in slowly, but at least the story was shaping up. If he spent most of the time writing, apart from this garden party thing tomorrow, he should have a decent number of chapters done to take with him to meet with his new editor on Tuesday. Thinking about the meeting reminded him he still had to find a way of getting to Brisbane. It was the last thing he wanted to do.

As Georgie sat back down, Liam walked across from the oven and placed a tray of pizza slices in the middle of the table. "Is there somewhere close by where I can rent a car?"

Georgie shook her head. "No. The closest car rental place is up at Noosa. At the Ritz-Carlton hotel."

"What about a taxi service? Is there one of those?" Liam frowned. He'd spent all night convincing himself he wasn't going to let her get under his skin, but even in her work clothes with her hair pulled back, she was beautiful, and he couldn't keep his eyes off her.

"Aldo, one of the retired locals, runs a service in Maleny," Georgie said.

"I have to go to Brisbane on Tuesday to meet with my editor."

"Aldo will be at the party tomorrow. I'll introduce you—"

Sienna interrupted her before she'd finished speaking. "You won't have to do that. Georgie's going down to the city on Tuesday to organise—"

Georgie cut her off. "Yes, I'd forgotten I have to go up to the city. I can drop you off at the car rental place."

"Thanks. I'd appreciate the ride." Liam's gaze stayed on Georgie and she held it steadily. Her expression was closed and he wondered whether she really wanted to run him up the coast. "But if it's a problem for you, I can see the taxi man tomorrow. Aldo?"

"No, no. I'd be happy to take you." She shook her head with a smile and his chest clenched. All he wanted to do was reach over and slip his hand through her hair, cup the back of her neck, and breathe in her sweet scent.

God, he had it bad. He reached for a slice of pizza to occupy his hands. Georgie had the same idea, and their fingers brushed as they both reached for the same slice.

She pulled her hand back as though she'd been burned. "I'd appreciate the company. So long as you can put up with the rattle of Ana's old truck."

"Thanks. I'm going to owe you for ferrying me around. I'd forgotten how far this house was from town." He put a slice of pizza on his plate before lifting the tray and holding it out to Georgie. "I'm going to buy a car after I meet with my editor on Tuesday."

Sienna looked at him with interest and he turned to her. "You knew the area around here before you bought the house, then?"

"Yes, I used to visit here with my grandmother when I was a child. I always loved the house, and when Uncle Joe died, I decided to buy it."

"*Uncle* Joe?" Georgie's voice was almost a squawk as her head flew up and her eyes locked with his. "Joe Humphries was your uncle?"

"A sort of uncle. He was my grandmother's cousin, and we came out to visit a couple of times when I was a kid. I don't know what it was, but something had happened in his life. Gran and I stayed with him one summer when I was about twelve."

Sienna laughed. "God, wait till Mitzi and Thelma hear that. You'll make their day."

"You know what?" Liam frowned. "Now that I think about it, I'm sure I remember that pink

Fireflite parked in the garage when I was a kid."

Sienna frowned. "I wonder why he left it to Mitzi and not to your family?" Georgie took the opportunity to study Liam's face as he turned away from her to face Sienna. He must have shaved last night, as only a hint of stubble shadowed his chin today. His eyes were alight with curiosity, and she took a deep breath as that hollow pang, the same one that had been there all night, came back and lodged in her stomach.

"He was in the war in Vietnam. His will stipulated that he wanted the house sold and the proceeds to go to a returned soldier's home. I was looking for somewhere to buy at the time, and it was perfect for what I wanted." Liam frowned. "I remembered that the car was to go to someone in town. I didn't make the connection till the two dears turned up here in the Fireflite in case they thought I should have it."

"Ooh, I do love a mystery. We'll have to dig, hey, Georgie?" Sienna elbowed her and Georgie glanced at her watch.

"What we have to do is get back to work." Georgie lightened her words with a smile. "I want you to get on to those fancy edges this afternoon and teach me how to do it so I can finish the rest when you're gone." She stood and pushed her chair back and began to clear the table. "I'll go home and check on Mutt.”

“Leave the dishes. I’ll clean up. Why don’t you bring Mutt back up here, if it’s easier? He was fine the other day.” Liam took the dishes from her and she was careful not to touch his fingers.

Sienna pushed her chair back. “You stay here. I want to go and get my phone. I left it in my room. Jack’s probably been trying to call me all morning. I’ll check on Mutt for you while I’m down there, too. If it looks like he’s tried to escape I’ll bring him back up with me.” She disappeared through the door before either of them could answer.

A prickle of discomfort flitted across the back of Georgie’s neck now that they were alone, and she looked down at her boots. “Ah, I’ll go up and get to work then. Lots to do.” She was terrified Liam would come over and hold her, and she was equally terrified he wouldn’t. Confusion filled her and she willed her feet to move, but they seemed to be stuck to the old-fashioned black-and-white checked tiles on the kitchen floor. “Thanks for lunch. I’ll get out of your way.”

Her words ran together in a rush and finally her feet came unstuck and she took off for the door. She almost made it when a warm hand touched her elbow. Liam must have moved quickly and quietly; she hadn’t been aware of him following her.

“Georgie, wait.” His voice sent a shiver down

her back to join the butterflies in her stomach.

She turned slowly and looked down at his long fingers now gently wrapped around her wrist.

"Yes." She lifted her gaze to his face. "Was there something you wanted?" *Stupid, stupid question.*

"No, I just wanted to ask what time you wanted to leave tomorrow." Crushing disappointment roared through her as he dropped his hand, and she raised her glance to his face. A small smile played about his lips, and she was scared he could read her mind.

"Tomorrow?"

"Yes, tomorrow for the…er…garden party thing." He laughed. "I've never been to a garden party before, let alone one that's being held in my honour. You'll have to tell me what the dress code is."

"The dress code?" *God, I must sound like a parrot, repeating everything he says.* She took a deep, calming breath and smiled at him. "Oh, you mean what to wear? Thelma and Mitzi will expect us all to dress up. They lean toward the side of formality. Not quite a tux"—a nervous laugh escaped her lips—"but certainly not too casual. Especially for the guest of honour. "Just wear whatever you wear to a book signing and come over to the cottage about noon." She shot him a smile, slipped through the doorway, and ran upstairs as quickly as she could.

To her relief, he didn't follow her, and a short while later she heard the study door close.

Chapter Twelve

By the time Sienna had put the decorative edges on the completed shelves and shown Georgie how to do it, the sun was hovering above the horizon and they had to turn the lights on as the room got darker.

"Why don't you close in the bottom and make cupboards for the base?" Sienna stood back and tipped her head to the side. "If you did the whole back wall as a cupboard base, it would balance the room. How about I go down and get Liam and see what he says?"

"No." Georgie shook her head. "He didn't want to be bothered. He just said to build whatever I want."

"He's been conspicuous by his absence this afternoon." Sienna pointed to the bag she'd brought back with her after lunch with a sheepish look on her face. "I thought he might sign my books for me."

Georgie put her hands on her hips and frowned. "Nuh-uh. Remember, he's the client. We're here to do a job. You can't be bothering him. It wouldn't be right."

"For goodness' sake, Georgie, the *client* cooked us lunch, and he *was* coming for dinner last night. And you were in a clinch with him in the backyard! Are you saying that because you're trying to avoid him? That speaks to me of an attraction."

Georgie ignored Sienna's question and began packing up her tools. Sienna knew her too well, and she was way too close to the truth.

Sienna huffed impatiently and walked across to pull the windows closed. "Come on. I won't mention him again."

"Good."

There was no sign of Liam when they left the house apart from a strip of light beneath the study door, and Georgie led Sienna quietly through the front door and closed it behind them. They looked at each other as the mournful howls of Mutt greeted them as they walked down the hill in the fading light.

"I should have taken Liam up on his offer."

Georgie grinned as the howls got louder. "That dog's so naughty."

The resulting giggles broke the uneasiness between them and they had a relaxing night talking and catching up, but studiously avoiding any further mention of Liam. Georgie was grateful that Sienna knew when to pull back. All she had to do was survive the garden party, where the matchmakers were sure to pool their resources, but she would be on her guard.

***

But Georgie wasn't quick enough the next day. Sienna deployed her first tactical move before they even left. Georgie glared at her cousin as Sienna slid from the bench seat of the car just as Liam was about to get in.

"Oh, silly me." Sienna put her hand to her cheek. "I left my phone inside. You slide across next to Georgie, Liam, and I'll sit by the window after I get it."

Sienna had already packed her bag and placed it in the back of the truck. Jack was picking her up from the party on his way back from the airport. Georgie shook her head. She was sure Sienna was using her phone as an excuse to get Liam in the middle of the seat and sitting next to her. It was as though they were teenagers again, trying to manoeuvre things so that they could sit beside the current hot guy on the school bus. As soon as she got Sienna alone, she'd tell her to back off. The last thing Georgie wanted was anyone interfering, even if they thought they were helping her out. It was bad enough that the day was going to be spent avoiding the matchmaking efforts of Thelma and Mitzi. Though since she knew exactly what to expect from them, she was prepared.

Sienna hurried purposefully toward the house and Liam slid in next to Georgie. She waved her hand around and gestured to the floor. "Watch out where you put your feet. I wiped the seat down for you but there's still a mess on the floor. Sorry."

"Sorry again?" He grinned at her, and this

time she was ready for the warmth that radiated through her chest.

"Yep. Sorry." She turned the key and the truck's old motor rattled to life. They sat for a moment without speaking and waited for Sienna to come back. The silence lengthened until it was uncomfortable. Georgie drummed her fingers on the steering wheel and cleared her throat as she peered through the windshield. "Sorry about the noise. Even though Ana doesn't use it much these days, it is a ute."

Finally, Sienna came out of the cottage and locked the door, but her hands were empty. Georgie shifted the truck into reverse and glanced into the rear view mirror before turning to Sienna. "Find your phone?"

"It must be in my bag in the back," Sienna said, smiling innocently.

Liam moved along the seat. It was only a small cabin with one bench seat, and by the time the truck began to move, his thigh was pressed hard against hers.

Thank goodness I wore long pants. Georgie had taken extra care with her appearance today. After all, one had to look the part to welcome a famous author into their small community. It didn't have anything to do with wanting to look her best because it was Liam.

As for him, Georgie's breath had caught in her throat when he'd walked through the gate. He was dressed in light-coloured pants with a long white shirt hanging loosely over them. Forget Mr. Darcy, he could have been a model for a fashion magazine. His hair was caught back behind his neck with a leather tie and he hadn't shaved. He had a dark blue sweater thrown casually over his shoulders, and Georgie had had to close her mouth when he came through the gate. Sienna had let out a soft sigh and murmured, "Yum. I might have Jack to go home to, but that sure doesn't stop me from looking." She'd fanned herself. "Ooh, he comes close to the best-looking man I've ever seen. The picture on the back of his books doesn't do him justice."

"All we need is a wet shirt and our dreams would come true," Georgie had muttered with a reluctant grin.

Now Liam's leg was pressed up against Georgie's loose silk trousers and her mouth dried. The warmth travelled upward from her thigh, and her skin tingled.

Thank goodness it's not too far to go.

She concentrated on driving while Sienna engaged Liam in conversation as they drove up the mountain. Cliff Cottage Thelma and Mitzi lived on the edge of town, so it was only a short while before she turned the truck onto Main Street, past the hardware store, to where Main Street turned into an unpaved road and meandered through the vegetable farms.

"It's like being out in the country," Liam commented, as Georgie parked the car on the road outside the old farmhouse.

She pulled on the hand brake and turned to him with a smile, determined to keep her cool. "You are in the country. Even though we're not far from the Sunshine Coast, the Maleny Chamber of Commerce does all it can to preserve the old feel of this town."

Liam smiled at her as she opened the door. "I like it. It has a nice vibe."

Georgie laughed as she slid from the car. "Let's see if you still feel that way after an afternoon in Thelma and Mitzi's clutches."

***

Liam sauntered along with Sienna as Georgie charged ahead of then. He was fast getting the impression that Georgie really wanted to hand him over to someone else. That would suit him fine. Being around her was not a good idea. As usual, he was having trouble focusing on anything else when she was in his sight. Her long legs were covered with some sort of soft green fabric and a cropped lace top beneath a shawl showed an occasional glimpse of bare skin at her waist. Her loose copper curls cascaded down her back and as he lowered his gaze, he didn't intend it to linger quite so long on the soft curves of her bottom displayed by the slinky fabric.

"Will you?" Sienna was looking at him and he realised he'd been totally immersed in looking at Georgie and hadn't heard her question.

"Will I what? Sorry, I was miles away." He stopped as Sienna took his arm.

"I said, Georgie is pretty fragile at the moment, and I asked you not to hurt her." Her face was serious and she looked back at him steadily.

"I don't intend to." Liam's body tensed defensively.

"Look, Georgie would kill me if she knew what I was saying, but you'd have to be blind not to see the sizzle sparking between the pair of you. She's had a few rough weeks and she's vulnerable, so if you are just looking for a quick roll in the hay, back off."

Her lips were pursed and her eyes were dark as she stared at him.

"I won't hurt her. I can promise you that." Liam didn't know where he was going with these feelings that seemed to take over whenever she was within his sight, but he certainly didn't intend to hurt her. God knows, he didn't want to put himself or anyone else through more emotional turmoil. He'd had enough of that to last him a lifetime. And if he was sensible, that should be warning enough for him to fight this crazy attraction that seemed to be consuming him. "I'm here to work, but I am also here to stay."

"Good, so we know where we all stand." She flashed him a grin, as though they hadn't just had such a serious conversation. "Now brace yourself."

Liam looked ahead as Sienna led him through a high arch covered with the yellow roses. A large garden, full of people, opened up in front of them. Even though it was almost winter, touches of colour still tinged the trees hanging along the fence line and a riot of bright flowers filled the garden beds. The familiar fragrance of orange blossoms drifted over to him and he looked for Georgie, but she'd already made her way across to a large group of people sitting near the house. He realised there was a small fruit orchard outside the fence and the orange blossom fragrance was drifting in on the soft breeze. A dozen large tables were covered with snow-white cloths, and a table along the back wall of the quaint little cottage was filled with food. Two elderly women, dressed in old-fashioned black-and-white outfits, moved through the crowd with a tray of drinks.

"Welcome to a Thelma and Mitzi 'do.'" Sienna grinned impishly at him. "You're in for a treat."

Liam shook his head as she led him past a couple of tables filled with various craft objects. Coloured rugs, crocheted doilies, and an assortment of knickknacks he had never seen before, and had no idea of their purpose, were crammed onto the table.

"It's like a country fair." He watched as an elderly woman behind a table laden with bottles wrapped up a bottle of fruit preserves and put the money in the pocket of her voluminous apron.

"It's like nothing else you'll ever see again." Sienna's face was alight with laughter but Liam was looking for Georgie. He caught a glimpse of her bright hair through the crowd and after muttering a quick excuse to Sienna, he followed her. He assumed Georgie had gone to the hostesses and he should thank them for inviting him. By the time he caught up to her, she was standing beside a tall thin man. Liam hung back, watching her smile as she chatted with the older man, who was beaming down at her. She caught sight of Liam and he noticed the moment she lost her composure. Satisfaction filled him with a warm glow. So, no matter what she said, she was certainly unsettled by his presence.

And that pleased him.

"Uncle Renzo. This is our guest of honour, Liam Wyndham." She turned toward the man with a look of pride. "Liam. This is my uncle."

"Ah. I have heard much about you. Welcome

to our community." Renzo pumped his hand vigorously and before Liam could speak, Georgie flitted off to another group.

Liam shrugged an apology to Renzo and followed her. "Excuse me."

Thelma and Mitzi were sitting at the table Georgie was heading toward, and when they spotted him, they both jumped to their feet. Before Georgie could take off again, he put his hand on her wrist and whispered to her with a grin.

"Don't leave me. Please?"

"Why? You're the guest of honour. Don't spoil their fun. They're going to want to take you around and introduce you to everybody. You're the celebrity in town." When she looked up at him, her eyes were dancing. "In fact, I think you're the first celebrity we've ever had.

"Though we did have the national champion pumpkin grower from the Gympie Pumpkin Festival here last year. He was here to tell us about the great pumpkin roll up at the Ecca." She tipped her head to the side with a little giggle. "But I don't think that compares with your adventures in Nepal. Everyone's so looking forward to hearing about them."

"Oh. God. Please don't tell me they're expecting me to give a talk." Dismay filled him as Georgie looked at him and then burst into laughter.

"I hate public speaking. Can't I just wave

hello to everyone from afar?" he said.

"No, that wouldn't be fair. Half the folk here are deaf and the other half would have trouble seeing you."

"Really? How long will we have to stay?"

He hadn't been too thrilled about coming, and now it seemed that the occasion was going to be just as bad as he'd imagined.

A final giggle escaped her and Georgie put her hand on top of his on her arm. "I'm just teasing you. You don't have to give a talk."

He groaned. Thelma and Mitzi were marching toward them with purpose in their step.

"But there will be a book signing." Liam loved the teasing glint that came into Georgie's eyes, even though he knew it was directed at him.

"A book signing?" He looked down at her and his eyes fixed on her lips as she smiled and nodded.

"Yes, a book signing. And now here come Thelma and Mitzi to whisk you away." She gave him a gentle shove in their direction, but before Georgie could step away, he reached back and grabbed her hand and gripped it tightly.

"Oh, no, you don't." He leaned over and whispered into her ear, gratified by the shiver that rippled through her. "I need company. I'm not doing this by myself."

"But I have to help with the food." She stared back at him wide-eyed.

"I'll help you do whatever it is you have to do. That way I can meet more people." He kept a firm grip on her hand until she stopped trying to pull away. It was nice having her fingers curled in his. This country atmosphere must be rubbing off on him.

Thelma and Mitzi descended on them; there was no other way to put it. The sisters bustled across the lawn, both dressed in long dresses and woollen shawls, and sporting large sunhats that were trimmed with lace and tied beneath their chins with coloured ribbon. Liam noticed the significant look the two women exchanged as they spied Georgie's hand firmly clutched in his.

"Welcome, dear boy." He was enveloped in a cloud of overpowering rose perfume as each of them kissed his cheek, both taking care not to step between him and Georgie. Looks like he had some support there, although he wasn't sure what he wanted to do about it. He was also aware of her uncle watching them from across the garden with an intent expression on his face.

Thelma and Mitzi each blew a kiss in Georgie's direction, and her hand moved in his grip as she went to greet them.

"How do you want me to help, ladies?" She wriggled her fingers again but he was not letting her go, squeezing them tighter as she shot him a glare. "How about in the kitchen? Looks like there are a few here for lunch?"

"No, no." The shorter of the two, who he now knew was Mitzi, shook her head. "You're in charge of the guest of honour this afternoon. We've got plenty of help."

"You show him around and we'll call you when it's time to eat." Thelma glanced down at their hands and winked at Georgie. Liam could almost feel the heat radiating off her face and neck as the blush stained her cheeks.

"I hope you don't mind, but we told everyone to bring their copy of your books and you might be happy to sign them?" Thelma pointed to the tables and he noticed there was one with a pile of books in the middle and a small queue forming already. "And we also bought some more for those who didn't have a copy already."

This time it was Georgie's turn to gloat, and she nudged him in the ribs as the two women headed back toward the house. Liam took the opportunity of slipping his arm around her waist as she leaned toward him.

"What are you doing?" she whispered.

"Making sure you don't leave me to face all of these strangers alone."

She frowned at him and he looked down at

her as she spoke. "I hope you understand you are setting us up for every gossip in town."

"Sticks and stones, and all that." It was all he could do not to kiss her, no matter who was watching. That would really keep the town talking. But he saw the look of distress on Georgie's face as she pressed her lips together before he could give in to the temptation, and he pulled back.

"Sorry, you deserved to be teased after you've had your fun. Come on. Do what you're supposed to do and introduce me to my new neighbours."

Five minutes later she'd introduced him to a bevy of folk and Liam had his free hand pumped a dozen times, not to mention the number of kisses bestowed on his cheek from women who were old enough to be his grandmother. Come to think of it— he looked around—Sienna and Georgie were the youngest here, by many years. It was almost as though they'd entered an aged care home.

He finally let her hand go and he settled at the table, signing his name for more readers than he ever imagined he'd find in such a small town.

When he said as much to Georgie, who had agreed to stay at the table, introduce him, and help with the books, she'd stared back at him and grinned. "We're not that far from civilisation."

He smiled at the next woman in the queue,

and wrote "To Dorothy" with a flourish when Georgie introduced her. Before the next book was placed in front of him, he murmured to her, "I wasn't having a go at you about the town. I'm just surprised so many of them actually have a copy of this book."

Georgie just smiled. After the next reader was introduced, had her book signed, and wafted away in a cloud of yet another floral perfume, he leaned back in the chair.

"Enjoying yourself?" Georgie looked back at him and her smile was still in place. Her fair skin was tipped with a soft pink blush on her cheekbones and her eyes were alight with something. Whatever it was, he'd like to keep that look on her face forever.

Liam realised he was enjoying himself. For the first time in many months, the heavy fog of sadness that had been with him since his marriage ended and Vanessa died had lifted, and he was feeling good. Even at the beginning of their relationship, he'd never been this relaxed in Vanessa's company. From the early days of their marriage, it had been very clear that she was not going to be happy with his company alone. They always had to be somewhere they would be *seen.*

Liam grinned. Vanessa would not have appreciated a garden party miles from the social scene in Sydney—let alone one where his face was the only famous one in sight. His contentment had more to do with being in Georgie's company than being out with a nice group of people on a glorious winter afternoon. He'd never let his guard down so quickly with anyone before. Her green eyes held his and her eyebrows rose as he nodded.

"Yes. Yes, I am."

"Why do you sound so surprised?" She tipped her head to the side and put down the book she was about to push across to him.

Liam was silent. There was a break in the book-signing line, and he and Georgie were by themselves. He wasn't going to screw this up, and he spoke slowly. "Are you?"

"Am I what? Surprised?" He watched as the tip of Georgie's tongue licked her bottom lip.

Slowly. Go slowly. Don't kill this mood.

"No, are you enjoying yourself?" She didn't answer, and Liam reached over and lifted her hand, looking at her pink-painted fingernails as he sought the right words. Chatter buzzed around them but they were alone at the table.

"Yes, I am. For the first time in quite a while, actually." Georgie looked back at him. "But don't read too much into that."

The words hung in the air between them. "What should I read into it?"

Georgie smiled sadly. "I guess you're just someone else who needed a little bit of pushing to feel a bit happier and maybe I've helped you…with this." She gestured around to her friends as laughter and happy conversations washed over them, though it seemed as if they were cocooned in a world of their own. "I'm good at that," she said and her voice was sad.

Never before had he felt this connected to another person as her eyes locked with his. "You know it's more than that. Admit it." Liam kept his voice low, and he reached up and brushed his fingers gently over the soft skin of her cheek. "Will you come to my place tonight for dinner and we can talk about it some more?"

Before Georgie could answer, Liam looked up as a woman stood behind Georgie and put her finger to her mouth in a shushing motion. A short man with a shiny bald head stood beside her and beamed as she put her hands over Georgie's eyes from behind.

"Guess who's home?" The woman leaned down and Georgie turned with a shriek.

"Magda!"

Any chance of further conversation disappeared as Georgie jumped up from her chair and embraced the couple. Liam watched as she grinned and introduced them to him.

"Liam, this is Joe and Magda. They used to own the hardware store, but now they spend most of their time cruising in the Pacific, or the Bahamas, or the Hawaiian Islands." Her face was alight, and unfamiliar warmth took him unawares.

"And I hear it's your turn next?" Magda held Georgie close and Liam's interest was piqued as she spoke softly. "We heard all about that silly stuff with Marietta. Are you and Sienna okay?" He moved away; whatever they were talking about was none of his business.

Her turn? Gossip had gotten around quickly. Magda appeared to assume they were a couple already.

"Everything's good. I'll come and visit you next week and fill you in. Okay?" Georgie turned to Liam. "Now I'm sure Joe would love to take one of your books on their next vacation." Liam frowned as Georgie reached beneath the table and pulled up another copy of one of his books.

She grinned at him with a sheepish expression. "Thelma bought all of the copies of your books she could find at the Maleny bookshop and told everyone they had to buy one. She said it was the best welcome the town could give you."

Liam rolled his eyes. "She didn't have to do that."

"They wanted you to feel at home." A little smile played about those gorgeous lips. "And besides, they tell me it's not a bad story."

She pushed the book to Liam and passed him the pen.

"Later," he mouthed to her before he picked the pen up, and was gratified to see the blush that stained her cheeks.

Chapter Thirteen

Georgie made good her escape while Joe engaged Liam in conversation. Apparently, Joe was already a fan of Liam's and had read all of his books. He questioned him about some of the places he'd been while he was researching his stories. It sounded like he was very well travelled. As she would be soon. She slipped her arm though Magda's and walked inside with her, and tried not to feel Liam's eyes on her back the whole way.

Later? Later what? Could she cope with later? The banter between them at the book-signing table had been fun, but every time Liam had turned his attention—and his charm—to one of her old friends, Georgie's heart had beat a little faster. Every time he'd picked up the pen and his long slender fingers had signed the page, she'd recalled the feel of them caressing her neck, or brushing her cheek…or just touching her.

He'd rolled his sleeves up and she hadn't been able to take her eyes from his smooth, muscular forearms as he'd talked to the person who was waiting for him to sign her book. The quiet sullen man had disappeared and she was sure it wasn't just an act for his new readers. Liam had looked at her with the same expression that Jack looked at Sienna, and Blake looked at Ana. No man had *ever* looked at

173

her like that.

She had to get away. Not just away from him, or the party this afternoon, but away from here, before she fell in—fell into a big hole of feelings she didn't need or want.

She wasn't going to go near the L-word. She'd been hurt too often when she'd thought a relationship might be heading that way.

A relationship? Get real, we don't have a relationship. No matter what Liam said about having dinner and talking some more. No matter how he looked at her.

No way. Not going there. She was not leaving herself open for anything. Besides, he hadn't realised they'd still be here for dinner. Thelma and Mitzi's parties went all day and into the night.

Georgie hadn't even noticed that Magda had left her alone until she heard her chattering away to Thelma by the old stove in the kitchen. She walked over to the window above the sink and watched as Liam charmed another person waiting in line.

No more kisses. The first time they'd kissed in the study she'd been uneasy with the way she'd felt. The second time in the orchard, it had scared the living daylights out of her. The third time—if she let a third time happen—she'd probably melt into a useless puddle at his feet.

No way. It was not going to happen. No

dinner, no talk, no more kissing…nothing else, no matter how good it might be.

"Penny for your thoughts?" She jumped as Sienna leaned against the sink beside her.

"Just taking a break while Liam signs some more books." She forced a false gaiety into her voice. "The old gals have outdone themselves today. Lots of guests."

"Don't change the subject." Sienna sighed as she put her hand on Georgie's arm. "Liam's a good man. I hope you're not going to mess this up. It's a chance for you to be happy…finally."

"Happy? I'm going away, remember?" Georgie straightened, reached for a dish towel, and passed it to her cousin. "Help me with the dishes."

For a few moments she scrubbed vigorously at a pot that was soaking in the sink. "Just because you've fallen for Jack doesn't mean I have to do the same thing."

Sienna stared at her without speaking.

"Have you seen the way Liam looks at you? He can't take his eyes off you. And I saw the state you were in after he kissed you on Friday night." Sienna took the pot from her. "It's me you're talking to, sis. You can't kid me." A little grin crossed her face. "Not since Billy Stephenson kissed you in the back of the school bus and I knew it before you were even down the steps and off the bus."

"Okay, so you might be a teensy…just a teensy bit right, but I'm a coward. Maybe a few months ago I would have risked it…but not now. I've decided that independence is my mantra. No more dreams of wedding dresses and houses with little white fences." Georgie clenched her jaw and shook her head. "But he wants me to go for dinner and I've decided I will. That's all it is."

"Good." Sienna put the dish towel on the bench and smiled at her.

"No, not good. I'm going to make it clear to Liam, once and for all, that I'm not available." Georgie folded her arms across her chest. "I've only got a few weeks before I go away and then I'll find out how to be happy on my own, without a man in my life. I cannot risk being dumped one more time. If I don't get together with him, he can't leave me, can he?"

***

Jack arrived late in the afternoon and Liam hung with him for a while. They helped carry platters of roast meat and baked vegetables out to the garden, and then Mitzi appeared with a bottle of homemade elderberry wine. Jack raised his eyebrows and sniffed it once it was uncorked.

"Not bad." He poured a glass for Liam and lifted his own glass in a toast. "Welcome to the Sunshine Coast. I hope you find it as wonderful here as I have."

Liam sipped the wine and was pleasantly surprised. There'd been a lot of surprises today. He nodded at Jack and lifted his own glass. "Thank you. So far the move has been pretty good."

For most of the afternoon, Liam had watched Georgie flutter around and look after the elderly folk. She'd brought them cups of tea and settled blankets over their legs as the chill of the late afternoon had settled in, and she hadn't stood still for one moment. She'd managed to avoid him for most of the time, despite the curious looks a couple of the women had thrown her way as she'd scurried past him. As for him, he'd had to concentrate on not looking at her the whole time. It was like being back at high school with the heart palpitations and the eye contact, focusing on the pretty girl who'd caught your attention.

He'd been pleased when Jack had sought him out and they'd spent some time getting to know each other during dinner.

Dinner. Not quite what he'd planned, but Georgie still had to run him home at the end of the night, and he intended to have a good talk to her before he let her go. He pushed away the thought that kept creeping into his head. *Slow down.*

"Sienna says you're buying a car this week?" Jack slipped his arm around Sienna's waist as she came up and stood by his chair. Liam looked around for Georgie. She was back in the kitchen helping clean up, and as he watched through the window she lifted her hair from her neck and wound it into a topknot on her head. The soft, silky fabric she was wearing slid up her arms and the light caught her bare skin as she stretched. His knees felt weak suddenly, and he switched his attention back to Jack.

"Yeah, I've been making some enquiries, but I won't be able to pick it up for a couple of weeks." Jack launched into a discussion of motor sizes and fuel consumption, but Liam kept one eye on the door, waiting for Georgie to come and join them. Finally, she wandered out and looked around the garden. He beckoned to her, before she could head off in another direction to help someone else, or clear a table, or just generally avoid his company.

She stood beside him as she greeted Jack.

Liam stood and leaned over to her, speaking quietly so he didn't appear rude. "What time do you want to leave?"

This whole afternoon with the Maleny community had been fun, and he'd enjoyed himself much more than he'd expected. They'd also stayed hours longer than he'd anticipated and he was beginning to get anxious about getting back to his study.

The sun had gone down and the flickering

lights shining over the garden burnished the copper colour of Georgie's hair. She'd removed the clip and her long auburn curls fell over the shawl she'd put around her shoulders before she'd come outside. The wind had picked up and there was a hint of rain in the air as the clouds swirled in.

"Soon." She yawned and covered her mouth with her hand. "Oops, sorry. It's past my bedtime."

"Mine, too," he said softly and grinned as she coloured up.

Good, keep her guessing.

There was a flurry to pack up the garden, and he and Jack helped carry the furniture into an old shed behind the house as the last of the food was carried inside. Finally, they made their farewells and as he thanked Thelma and Mitzi for inviting him, they presented him with a pumpkin pie. Georgie was quiet as they walked out to the street with Jack and Sienna to get Sienna's bag from the ute, and she didn't speak even as Sienna hugged her good-bye.

Georgie opened the car door and slipped onto the bench seat and waited for him as Liam shook Jack's hand and kissed Sienna's cheek before getting into the truck. He was looking forward to getting to know them more. As he climbed in, she was rubbing her hands up her arms and shivering.

So much for my plan to be a recluse. The community had made him feel welcome, and as far as Georgie went, his desire for privacy had flown out the window. It suited him and it seemed like he'd chosen the right place to put roots down.

"Too breezy?" He waved as Sienna's red sports car passed them but kept his gaze on Georgie.

"A little."

Liam wound the window up and looked at the dashboard in front of him as she started the car. "Would you like me to put the air on?"

"It's broken." Finally, a glimmer of life appeared on her face as she shot him a smile. "Don't worry, home's not far."

The first raindrops splattered on the windshield as she turned off the motorway onto the shared road that led to both of their houses.

"Don't worry about going up to my place. Park at your house and then I know you're inside safely. This weather is closing in quickly." Liam leaned forward as a flash of something caught his attention on the top of the cliff. "I'll walk up the hill."

Georgie groaned as there was another movement ahead of them. "Oh, no. That was Mutt. He's gotten out again." She accelerated and turned into her drive at the bottom of the hill. The engine stopped with a shudder as she turned the key, but she left the headlights on.

"I'll help you find him." Liam opened his door. The rain had started to fall in earnest now and cold needles of ice hit his bare neck. "I'll call him while you get an umbrella."

He didn't wait for her to answer as he slid from the truck and ran to the path at the top of the cliff where he'd last seen the dog.

"Be careful. Don't go too close to the edge. It's soft." Georgie was right behind him and he reached back and held out his hand.

"What about the umbrella?" he asked.

"No time. If that blasted dog gets down onto the beach, he'll run for miles."

Liam smiled to himself as Georgie slipped her hand into his, and they followed the sandy path lit by the headlights.

"Mutt! Get back here."

Liam whistled as Georgie called out and they were rewarded with a scuffling noise a short distance ahead of them. She stopped and put her hand up. "Wait up. If we keep walking, he'll think we are going down to the beach."

"In the dark?" Liam peered ahead but couldn't see the dog, nor could he hear it any more.

"He's not real smart." He could hear the grin in Georgie's voice, despite the rain that was getting heavier by the minute. Water was beginning to trickle down beneath the collar of his shirt, but he didn't care.

He squeezed her hand as they kept walking.

He was beginning to love this dog.

Chapter Fourteen

A litany of swear words was running through Georgie's head and she bit her lip to stop them from coming out of her mouth.

Blasted dog.

"Mutt, come here!" Her voice cracked as she attempted to call the dog back to them. They stood at the top of the cliff where the path ran down to the beach. She shivered as a trickle of cold water ran down the side of her face, and then she trembled again as Liam's arm went around her waist to pull her close to him.

"You should have gotten that umbrella," he said.

"I didn't have time."

The rain pelted them more heavily as he spoke; it was as though the heavens were having a laugh at their expense. As she peered into the dark at the end of the path, a very wet dog slunk toward them, his tail firmly between his legs. Georgie reached down and looped her fingers through his collar. The smell of wet dog drifted up to her as he shook himself and water droplets went flying around them.

Liam laughed. "Well, at least we're already wet." His arm was still firmly around her waist and he reached down with the other to hold Mutt's collar. "I've got him. Where do you want to put him?"

Georgie let go of the dog and straightened, blinking the water from her eyes as she looked up at Liam. The light from the car was shining directly onto his face and his eyelashes were clumped together in spikes as he stared back at her.

"He'll have to come inside because I can't risk him getting out again tonight. You take him onto the porch and I'll turn the car lights off." Liam let his arm drop and ran across to the porch with the dog as Georgie headed to the car. She grabbed her bag and Liam's sweater off the seat, and locked the door.

By the time she'd followed them onto the porch, deep rivulets from the heavy rain were running across the lawn. Her feet sloshed through ankle-deep water and she regretted the ruin of her favourite pair of shoes. Liam was waiting at the top of the steps.

"I'm glad the rain held off for the afternoon. I hope everyone got home safely," she said.

Liam grabbed for her as her wet shoes slipped on the top step and she almost fell. Mutt barked as she regained her balance and she frowned at him.

"It's your fault, you naughty dog." She reached up and brushed the wet bangs from her eyes with the back of her hand, and wrinkled her nose as the cloying aroma of wet dog hair hit her. "Come inside and bring him, too. He can go in the utility room and I'll dry him off."

The task of looking for Mutt had kept her mind focused, but as Georgie unlocked the door and turned the lights on, all the warm and trembling feelings came rushing back as Liam pushed the dog gently into the laundry room. Despite the moisture in the air, and her dripping hair and sodden clothes, her mouth dried at the sight of Liam bathed in the bright light.

Oh, Sienna! Who needed Mr. Darcy on the big screen when she had Liam Wyndham standing here in front of her?

Damn wet shirt. From the first moment she'd come across him lying on the wet sand, she'd known how good-looking he was. On top of the great looks, the sexy eyes, the muscular chest encased in the wet shirt that was filling her vision, she also knew what a nice guy he was.

Thoughtful, funny, and kind. And a great kisser.

Don't go there.

Gradually it dawned on Georgie that Liam was standing there grinning at her as she gaped up at him. The heat rushed up her neck and it was a wonder it didn't sizzle the water on her face as her cheeks burned.

"Have you got an old towel? I'll rub him dry

for you," Liam asked.

She took a step back and scrabbled through the cupboard, not knowing what was in there. Finally she pulled out an old drop cloth that they'd used to cover the furniture when they'd painted Ana's cottage a couple of years back, and she handed it to Liam. "This will have to do. I don't fancy using any of Ana's good pink towels to dry him off."

She leaned back on the doorframe and watched as Liam's hands rubbed the dog's wet coat with the stiff piece of fabric. The cloth softened as he stroked him up and down gently, and if it was possible for a dog to have an expression of ecstasy in its face, Mutt was wearing one. She'd have one on her face, too, if Liam's hand were moving on her body like that.

Don't think about it. She swallowed again.

The rain was still drumming down onto the shingled roof and Georgie could barely hear Liam's words as he turned to her. She leaned closer and heard him say something about getting warm, before he folded the drop cloth and placed it in the corner of the small room. Mutt flopped down onto it, curled into a ball, and promptly closed his eyes.

Liam gestured to the door and she stepped out onto the porch and he followed her, pulling the door of the laundry room shut behind him. The wind had picked up and the rain was driving almost horizontally in from the sea, and the tang of salt came from the droplets that settled on Georgie's face. She unlocked the front door and a gust of wind blew it open and it crashed into the wall.

"Quickly," she called to Liam to follow her and he pushed the door shut against the wind.

"I guess you're stuck with my company for a while." He lifted both his hands and pushed his hair back from his face, and Georgie slowly became aware of how bedraggled she must look. Her hair was in wet tangles and her fringe was stuck to her forehead. She looked down. Her lace top was sodden and stuck to her chest, moulding the curve of her breasts. Her silk pants stuck to her legs and her shoes were a pulpy mess of wet leather.

"This was one of my favourite outfits." She lifted her hands in the air and grinned at Liam. "But you don't look much better."

Actually he does, but there is no way I'm telling him that.

"You're soaked. Go up and dry off."

###

Georgie had a quick shower and dried her hair with the hair dryer before dressing in a pair of jeans and a cotton jumper. The wind and the rain were still beating against the upstairs windows, so it was clear Liam wouldn't be going back to his house any time soon. She grabbed a fresh towel and riffled though the spare room where she'd noticed some of Blake's clothes on a shelf when she'd been making the room up for Sienna. A pair of faded but neatly pressed Levis and a soft sweatshirt filled her arms as she walked slowly downstairs.

Tonight would be the perfect opportunity to make it quite clear to Liam that this attraction between them wasn't going to go anywhere. Her breath caught in her throat as she reached the bottom step. He was standing in front of a crackling fire holding his wet shirt up to the heat. As he raised his arms, the muscles in his back flexed and rippled, and Georgie's mouth dried. His long pants were still damp and moulded to his legs.

Even though it was almost summer, he'd lit a fire. The firelight flickered and patterns of light danced across the walls and she knew as soon as he turned to her, the shadowed room would only enhance those high cheekbones and the planes of his face that were becoming very familiar to her. Straightening her shoulders, Georgie flicked on the light switch on the wall at the bottom of the stairs and the room was bathed in bright light, dispelling any romantic scene he may have tried to set.

Liam turned slowly and a smile spread across his face as he spied the clothes and the towel in her arms. "For me?"

Georgie nodded, still not willing to trust her

voice. She walked over and stood beside him in front of the flames and cleared her throat. "If you'd like to use the bathroom upstairs, there's plenty of hot water."

Liam shook his head. "It's okay. I'll just dry off and get changed. As soon as the rain lets up I'll go home. I really must do some writing tonight."

"There's a small room over there where you can change." Georgie pointed to the door beside the kitchen, avoiding looking at his bare chest. "I'll make us some coffee while you get dried off. Would you like some pie to go with it?"

"No, thanks." Liam shook his head as he headed for the door. "I feel as though I've been eating all day."

"It's Thelma's pumpkin pie." She smiled at him. "Trust me, it's to die for."

"Okay, maybe just a small piece."

Great. So far so good. A normal conversation.

When he came back out dressed in a pair of jeans that hung loosely around his legs, and the old stained sweatshirt, Georgie busied herself in the kitchen. Liam walked back over to the fireplace and spread his wet clothes on the fire guard.

"Did you know that you can get a pumpkin beer at Maleny?' She placed the sugar and cream on a tray before she added one slice of pie to a plate.

"And there's pumpkin wine and pumpkin rum, too."

She glanced across at him as she carried the tray over and placed it on the low table next to the sofa. "You've got a good fire going there," she said briskly. "I might go out and get Mutt. He'd enjoy it in here. Sit down, make yourself at home." She plumped up the cushions. "So did you enjoy yourself today?"

A normal one-sided conversation. She was babbling, but she wanted to fill the room with everyday conversation. All she could think of was the "later" that he'd mouthed earlier. As she turned to go and fetch Mutt, Liam's warm hand gently touched her on the shoulder.

"Georgie?"

"Mmm?" She looked down at his bare feet.

"Forget Mutt…and stop talking."

Slowly she raised her eyes as he gently tucked a stray tendril of hair behind her ear. Her brain was slow to respond as her blood heated her faster than any fire could. "Stop talking?"

Liam dropped his hands and took both of hers between his. She looked down at her small hands enclosed between his slender white fingers. She loved his hands; she couldn't begin to imagine how much she'd love to feel them on her skin.

"Yes." He murmured as he lifted her hand to his mouth. "Just feel."

His warm lips touched the inside of her palm and Georgie closed her eyes as he spoke softly. "I told you I wanted to talk to you."

"Because I was teasing you?" She swallowed and opened her eyes and immediately regretted it. Liam's sexy blue eyes were fixed on her face.

"No. Because I want to sort out this…this thing between us." He uncurled his fingers from around hers and raised his hand to cup her cheek. His thumb brushed her skin ever so gently. "I'm not ready for this, but I can't get you out of my head. I want you to know how I feel but I want to be honest. I don't want to give you the wrong idea."

A little voice in her head was telling her to take this one night, enjoy being with him, and then she could worry about it later. *What was the wrong idea?*

No. Georgie knew she had to be strong, but as she opened her lips to speak, he moved his fingers from her cheek and brushed them against the sensitive skin at the nape of her neck before he gently cradled the back of head. Her resolve disappeared like the smoke that was puffing up the chimney.

One night. She could have one night. With a soft sigh she leaned forward and pressed her lips against his, and their breath mingled as he whispered against her mouth.

"You are so beautiful. You've bewitched me,

Georgie." She loved the way he rolled her name on his tongue. His whisper ran through her body as he pulled her close and his firm chest pressed against her breasts. Liam slid his lips across her cheek, his hand still cupping the back of her head. "Your green eyes, your gorgeous hair, your lips. I can't take my eyes off of you."

For the first time in her life, Georgie felt truly beautiful. Liam was worshipping her body with gentle hands. She closed her eyes as he ran those hands down her shoulders and caressed lazy circles on her back as his mouth moved on hers. This time the pressure was firmer and she opened her lips to welcome him. She arched her body into his as the sensuality of the moment consumed her.

They stood there for a long time, lost in a pleasure that was filled with soft breaths and deep sighs, until a log snapped with a loud *crack* in the fireplace. Georgie drew back slowly and reached her hand up to Liam's cheek. He turned his lips and kissed her palm again as she spoke. "I want to talk to you tonight. I want to tell you about me. I want to be honest with you." Her throat filled with emotion as he looked back at her with a gentle smile. No man had ever looked at her as though she was the most beautiful woman in the world, but she sighed. It was too late.

She turned away from him, trying to put a

brake on the feelings racing though her. "Our coffee will be cold."

Liam sat on the sofa and didn't take his eyes from her as she picked up the coffeepot. "What do you want to tell me?" He patted the sofa, and she sat next to him after she poured the coffee. Both cups sat untouched as he looked at her.

"It's all right, Georgie. I'm not going to make you go anywhere you don't want to." She lifted her eyes to meet his. "But I want you to know—"

"No, you don't need to tell me anything." Her voice caught on a breath and she cleared her throat. "I'm not good at relationships, and I've failed at them so many times I'm not going to risk it again. No matter how tempted I might be."

Liam picked up her hand and smoothed his thumb across the back of it. The jolt from his touch went straight to her heart. She had taken care of herself for long enough now to be able to resist a simple touch, and she closed her eyes as she fought the temptation to lean against him.

His soft voice interrupted her thoughts. "That makes two of us. I'm not good at relationships, either. In fact, I've recently had a mammoth failure. So what do you say? Can you have a casual relationship? Can we do this?"

No man had ever been so honest with her. And it was the first time in Georgie's life she'd gone in with her eyes open, expecting nothing. Expecting no permanent outcome; having no dreams of dresses and wedding cakes. She slid across the sofa to him, and the coffee was forgotten as she opened his arms to her.

"This?" she asked. "What is this?"

"I'll try to show you," Liam murmured as he lowered his lips to hers once more.

Chapter Fifteen

A mournful howl woke Georgie the next morning and she opened her eyes slowly, wondering what the heavy weight on her leg was. She tried to roll but she was pinned to the bed with two firm arms wrapped around her.

"I think Mutt wants to go out." Liam's lips were warm as he nuzzled them against her cheek. Georgie arched her neck and stretched her body as she sought the right words. She'd never been any good at the morning-after stuff.

"I'd better go and let him out." Self-consciousness flooded though her as she rolled over and reached for her jeans, which were in a pile of clothes on the floor. She waited for Liam to look away.

He grinned at her. "You're shy?"

She nodded but he didn't look away.

"You're beautiful." His eyes moved slowly down from her face to her shoulders as she stood and grabbed the sheet to cover herself.

This was crazy. How the heck did she ever get herself into this situation with Liam Wyndham—the famous Liam Wyndham—in her bed in her friends' cottage?

Grabbing her jeans and her sweatshirt, Georgie took off into the bathroom. She let the sheet drop and stared at herself in the mirror as she ran the faucets. Her cheeks were flushed and her eyes were heavy. They hadn't had much sleep. Slowly, she let the smile that was tugging at her lips spread over her face and she nodded as she pulled her clothes on.

A very satisfied woman looked back at her. Tapping into her newfound self-assurance, she sauntered back into the bedroom, her confidence buoyed now that she was fully clothed.

Which was more than she could say for the sexy man still lying in her bed.

Liam was on his back, hands tucked casually behind his head, which was resting on *her* lacy pillow cover.

"Get up, lazybones. I have a job to go to up the hill." She grinned down at him as he rolled over and reached for his watch on her bedside cupboard.

He groaned. "And I've got to go write. If I don't get those chapters written today, I won't have a house for you to build bookshelves in."

Before she could walk away, he grabbed her hand and pulled her down to the bed. "How about a good-morning kiss from you before you go see to that dog?"

Georgie's hand shook in his as she leaned down to meet his lips. This man was like a drug. No matter what her mind was telling her, her body was not listening.

She giggled as another mournful howl reverberated from below. "At least Mutt isn't disturbing the neighbours."

***

Liam looked around the small bathroom as he washed and dressed. There were little signs of Georgie everywhere, and that filled him with a warm glow. He had it bad. Never before had he grinned at a pair of women's work boots on the floor and a pair of dirty socks hanging over the bath.

By the time he'd dressed in the borrowed clothes and sauntered down the stairs, the smell of brewing coffee greeted him. Georgie was standing at the window looking over the ocean as she nibbled on a piece of toast. The sky was a brilliant blue and the sea was smooth after the storm. The world was washed clean and Liam watched as Mutt raced around the yard below with a piece of wood. Did everything look as bright as he thought, or was it the way he felt?

He stood behind Georgie and put his hands on her shoulders. "Morning."

"Gorgeous day." She leaned back into him.

"It is," he said as he lowered his head and nuzzled into the soft skin of her neck, disappointed when she moved away slightly.

"Do you mind if we go now? I'll pour you a coffee and you can bring it with you so you can unlock for me. I really need to get started."

"Can I have some pumpkin pie to go with it?"

"*Ugh.* For breakfast?" Georgie glanced down at her watch with a smile. "Come on, I have to get to work."

Liam laughed. "I'm the one with the deadline. I don't mind how long it takes you to build my shelves." He turned her around and looped his arms around her waist as an idea struck him. "In fact, when you finish them, how would you like to start work on the rest of the house?"

Her smile faded as she stared back at him. "It would be a fabulous job, but I won't be able to. I'm leaving on Christmas Eve."

"You can do it when you come back from your vacation?"

Disappointment filled him as Georgie's brow wrinkled and she shook her head.

"But I'm not coming back. I'm leaving Hideaway Bay."

Her words surprised her, but Georgie knew it was the only way to guard her heart.

***

Liam unlocked his front door and Georgie nodded her thanks to him. He'd offered to bring Mutt up with them and she thought it was more for him to have something to focus on so they didn't have to talk. When she'd mentioned moving on, he hadn't

198

commented. He'd dropped his arms and gone into the kitchen, and she heard the gurgle of the coffeemaker as he poured himself a coffee. She'd gone upstairs and changed into her work clothes and boots and shoved her mobile phone into her pocket.

The walk up to the house had been quiet, with each of them making desultory comments about the weather and the beautiful sapphire blue of the ocean. Mutt eased the tension by bounding from one to the other, but Georgie sensed that Liam's thoughts were elsewhere as he headed for his study and she went upstairs to work.

Probably on his book.

"Damn!" She swore as she hit her thumb with the hammer for the fifth time in three hours. Like Liam, her thoughts were elsewhere, but they weren't on his book or even on her upcoming trip. His face filled her mind. The night they'd shared had been magic. He was kind, considerate, loving, teasing, and damn beautiful to look at. Last night he'd opened up and let her into his soul, and she'd seen the creative side of him flow as he'd whispered softly to her. Words that brought them so close to each other, and words she would remember for the rest of her life.

If only… Georgie shook herself and willed herself to move on. She'd killed it all by telling him she was leaving.

I am leaving. Get the job done. Finish up and

move on. Independence.

She picked up a length of wood and pulled out her tape, measured it, and cut it to size. It was only when she carried it over to the wall and tried to fit it that she realised she'd cut it too short and too wide. She moved across to the window and sat on the ledge, letting the breeze cool her.

Had last night been a mistake? They both carried baggage and they both had things they wanted to achieve, plus she had places to go. They would have to come to terms with it and break it off before one of them—or both—got hurt. And God knew, neither of them could handle any more hurt. She'd just read about Liam and his ex-wife in a magazine that she was sure Sienna had left lying around deliberately.

While Sienna had been trying to matchmake, maybe she'd also wanted to make sure Georgie went in with her eyes wide open. Well, she had, but it was beginning to hurt already. The fear of leaving the Sunshine Coast was now real. She could almost taste the uncertainty building in her chest, and the thought of leaving Liam when she'd just met him was one she didn't like.

She closed her eyes but his face wouldn't go away.

His gentle smile, his blue eyes, and the angles of his face. She raised her hand to her own cheek—

it was still tender from the rasp of his rough stubble against her skin. The memory of how little sleep they'd gotten brought a smile to her face, and she opened her eyes as resolve flooded through her.

She was overthinking this…as usual. Georgie could almost hear Sienna's voice in her head. *"Stop analysing everything. Just enjoy the moment."*

Over the past few months, she'd forgotten how to have fun, how to enjoy life. She'd always been the one who had played the practical jokes and thought up the harebrained schemes when they'd been growing up. It was time to lighten up and retrieve her old sense of fun. She'd been the mistress of sending funny texts. Sienna had even threatened to print them out and publish them in a book.

There was no reason why she couldn't spend some time with Liam before she went away. Ana had Blake, Sienna had Jack, why couldn't she hook up with Liam and have some fun with him before she went away? Memories to hold on to while she was off learning how to be independent. Georgie grinned as she remembered some of the memories that had been made last night. Okay, if she'd been looking for the real thing, it might have worked out. He might have been the One… Now that she had planned out her life, though, she didn't need Liam.

But there was nothing to stop her from seizing the moment, was there?

Three more weeks. She might as well make the most of it. They'd have a good time and if they spent the odd night together, well, that would add some more amazing memories to take away with her. It was time to take what life offered her before she headed off into the big wide world.

And she was going to start right this minute.

Georgie stopped outside the door of the downstairs study and balanced the tray she was carrying on one arm. With the other hand she pulled the band from her hair, shook her hair loose, and licked her lips, trying to ignore the sudden lack of moisture in her mouth. Taking a deep breath for courage, she tapped lightly on the door before pushing it open.

As she walked across the room, Liam turned and his eyes crinkled at the edges.

Phew. First hurdle overcome.

"It's way past lunchtime." She kept her voice bright and busied herself finding a clear spot to put the tray down. "I made us some sandwiches." She grinned as she looked around at the piles of books on the floor. "You sure do need those bookshelves."

Liam jumped up, took the tray from her, and put it on his desk. He looked distracted, and for a moment she was worried that she'd intruded on his privacy. That worry disappeared when he reached out and pulled her to him. His hair was mussed as though he'd been running his hands through it, but his smile was sweet as he looked down at her.

"I was just thinking about coming up and telling you it was time for a break. You work too hard." He pulled her closer.

"Really? I thought—" But she didn't get to tell him what she thought because he was kissing her. Softly and gently, and Georgie slid her hands up beneath his shirt and splayed her fingers on the smooth skin of his back. Liam's mouth moved from her lips to her cheek and then to that ticklish spot on her neck beneath her ear. He'd discovered that last night and now he headed straight for it.

She couldn't help the giggle that bubbled through her lips.

"So you find my lovemaking amusing?" He pulled back and looked at her for a long moment. "Hmm. I must be out of practice. Maybe I'd better do something about that?"

"What about lunch?"

"Lunch?" His eyes were half closed, and the way he was looking at her sent a thrill shooting all the way to Georgie's toes. "Seeing as you've gone to all that trouble, we'd better eat…first."

The thrill turned into a shiver and Georgie swore that her entire body was covered in goose bumps.

***

The afternoon flew by in a very pleasurable manner, but Liam didn't spend it writing new chapters, and Georgie didn't build any new bookshelves. He propped himself up on one elbow and watched her as she stood looking out the window of his bedroom. She was wearing one of his white shirts and it just covered her bare thighs.

"I'd better go downstairs and check on Mutt. It's almost dark." She picked up her shorts and slid them up over those long legs with his shirt hanging out loose over them

"You made lunch, so I guess it's my turn to cook dinner?" Liam slid off the bed and reached for his jeans. "You will stay?"

"For dinner?" Georgie's beautiful green eyes held the hint of a smile.

"I was hoping for the night?" As she walked toward the door, he grabbed her hand and held it against his chest. Her cheeks were rosy and her skin was still damp with perspiration. Liam inhaled the sweet smell of her hair as she rested her head against his shoulder.

"Shouldn't you be writing?" Georgie asked. She was a perfect fit against him, and he slid his hand through her silky hair.

"I should be, but I've written enough to make my editor happy." The muse had come back with a vengeance, and the more time he spent with Georgie, the more the words flowed. "Very happy."

"Shoot, I forgot we were going to the city tomorrow." She pulled back with a frown. "I've hardly done any work today. What time is your appointment?"

"A lunchtime meeting at the Ritz. If it's a problem for you to take me there, I can call Aldo and get him to drive me down to Brisbane." He smiled when the tell-tale blush stained her cheeks and her frown disappeared. "But it would be nice to have your company."

"No, it's all good. I have to go up there, too. I just worry about getting your job finished. No matter what"—she looked at him coyly from beneath her lashes—"you are paying the store for me to build you a room full of bookshelves. I've made very little progress today."

"But it has been a good day?"

"You know it has. And I don't think you need any more practice for a while." Georgie's eyes held a mischievous glint as she moved away from him. "Now I'm going down to see to that poor neglected dog while you cook."

Liam sat down on the bed after she went downstairs. The sense of contentment that flowed through him was unfamiliar. He hadn't felt this at ease in a long time. He took a deep breath and basked in the warmth that was flowing through him. His book was coming along brilliantly, and he knew that Georgie was responsible for the way he was feeling and the way the words were appearing. She'd gotten beneath his skin and brought his emotions spiralling back to the surface.

The good ones.

If he kept writing like this, he'd have this book finished well before the Christmas Eve deadline. Georgie had brought a fresh outlook and joy into his life in the short time he'd known her. Even when he'd been with Vanessa, her neediness had stifled him.

The social life she had made for them had been time-consuming and had bored Liam. The joy that his writing had given him had disappeared as he realised the mistake he had made in marrying Vanessa—along with his muse. That had been the problem with his writing over the past few months. Events since her death had overwhelmed him, and it had continued to block his creativity. He'd buried his feelings and not let himself feel the emotions that were bubbling under the surface—the facade he showed to the world. The person he'd become in the artificial world she'd created for them.

But he still had work to do. *If I can drag myself away from Georgie and back to the computer.* And he had to sort out exactly what these feelings were. He'd only just met her, but in ten days she'd made him feel more alive than he'd felt in the last two years.

Liam frowned and made his way down to the kitchen, deep in thought.

Chapter Sixteen

Sex between two consenting adults.

That's all it was.

Nothing else.

Georgie cursed as her hair band snapped and her neatly coiled hair tumbled down. Good times before she went away.

They were going to be late. Even though she didn't have an appointment, she knew Liam had to be at the Fairmont hotel at noon to meet with his editor. It wasn't far from there to the travel agency on Queen Street, and it was a beautiful day for a walk.

Even though Liam had wanted her to stay the night, she'd insisted on coming home after dinner, telling him she had things to do, but she'd come home mainly because she'd needed some space. She did have to organise some dates and papers to take to the travel agency and she should have done it last night, but when Liam had insisted on walking her home, he'd come in and ended up staying and they'd talked until after midnight.

Georgie couldn't help grinning as she fixed her hair. She'd taken extra care with her appearance today. A touch of makeup, an elegant hairstyle—if only she could get it to stay up—and a long-sleeved silk top over black jeans. A pair of flat but strappy sandals completed the look. If she was spending at least part of the day in Liam's company, she wanted to look nice.

"Oh. Damn." A tap at the door announced his arrival and she opened her window and called down to him. "I'm coming." She gave up on her hair and gave it a quick brush, leaving it loose, checked her lipstick, and picked up her bag and travel itinerary.

Liam was waiting on the porch, stroking Ana's cat, Sooky, and Georgie's mouth dropped open as she pulled the door shut behind her.

"We...ell, Mr. Author, don't you look right pretty." She tipped her head to the side and looked him up and down. From the tip of his polished shoes to the neatly knotted tie at the collar of his pale blue business shirt.

"Not as pretty as you do." His smile sent a pleasant buzz through her and she smoothed her hair back from her face.

"It's a shame we have to climb into that old truck," she said.

Liam looked over at the truck and then glanced down at his watch. "I have an idea. We have plenty of time. My editor called just as I was leaving. Her flight's been delayed so my meeting's been put back till two o'clock. I hope that doesn't mess with your day?"

Georgie shook her head and waited to hear

his idea, but he smiled enigmatically without telling her what it was. She shrugged and called out to Mutt as she opened the door of the old ute. "You guard the house, boy, and don't even think about getting out."

"Will he be okay home by himself?" Liam frowned as he slid in beside her and a shot of warmth filled her. He really was a great guy, and she was getting more sucked in each time he did or said something sweet—and there had been more than a few of those times over the past couple of days.

"He should be okay. I got up early and checked the fence where he's been getting out and it looks sturdy. He might howl a bit but he'll be fine." She looked up with a grin at Liam's house perched on top of the cliff. "At least he won't bother the neighbours."

The Bruce Highway was busy, and Georgie concentrated on driving as they headed south. They were just past Caloundra when Liam's phone rang. Georgie turned off the motorway at the next exit while he answered. The ute was so damn noisy it was almost impossible to hold a conversation when it was speeding along the road, let alone hear someone on the other end of a mobile phone when the motor was revving away.

Liam shot her a smile as he took the call. They were parked on a bluff just before the golf club and the view of the sea opened out in front of them.

The birds were diving for fish close to the shore, and when Georgie opened her window, their shrill cries floated in on the sea breeze. It was a glorious day—no clouds and very little wind. Despite being early summer, the forecast was for the high twenties. The smell of the salt air was refreshing as it drifted up from the sea.

"Thank you, I'll wait for your email." Liam's words were formal and Georgie glanced over at him. A frown wrinkled his brow as he stared out through the windshield and he was unaware of her looking at him. Georgie made the most of the opportunity. He was clean-shaven this morning, and the angles of his face were less pronounced without the shadow of his usual dark stubble. His shirt was the same ice blue as his eyes and his hair curled softly onto the collar.

Georgie knew she was falling for him and that it was a crazy thing to do. She had to put a halt to it before she got hurt. And she knew that hurt would come as sure as morning followed night. It would be worse, much worse than any other time, because she'd never fallen so deeply for any other man. She sighed and turned back to the view over the ocean.

"No problem, it's not your fault. Talk soon." Liam disconnected and put the phone back on the seat between them.

"Change of plans," he said. "Larissa's flight

has been cancelled and she's postponed the meeting till next week."

"Oh." Georgie bit her lip. "So what do you want to do?" Did he want to go back home? They were only half an hour away and she'd have time to drive him back and still go down to Brisbane.

"Can you take a left here and go back to Caloundra?" Liam grinned at her and her stomach did a double backflip. If he'd asked her to fly to the moon with a smile like that, she would have done her damnedest to do it.

"Sure…where to?"

"Do you know where the Ritz-Carlton is?" He looked very pleased about something as Georgie started the car.

"Yes, it's the next left, overlooking the top of the island."

She followed the curving road until they reached the hotel. The yellow brick building perched on the sweeping lawns glowed in the morning sun. It was a beautiful place and Georgie had always had a yen to stay here. Liam grabbed his jacket and climbed out.

"I won't be too long, I hope."

Georgie shrugged and settled in to wait. Ana's old ute looked out of place next to all the flashy cars parked along the manicured hedge. She pulled out the folder holding her travel documents and began to think of the questions she had for Sandy, the travel consultant. She hadn't had a chance to think about her trip for a while. Either that or she was blocking it from her mind. The tentative itinerary was Hawaii to Rio de Janeiro after Christmas and in March she'd fly to California. She had to decide how long she would stay in San Francisco and then choose her next destination so Sandy could book her flights. Georgie flicked through some of the brochures the travel agent had sent her, but nothing appealed. She sighed and put her head back on the headrest. It was too late to change her mind; she'd paid for half of the trip already and changing her mind because she was a coward—or for some other reason she was not even going to think about—was not enough for the travel insurance company to refund her money.

The noise of her door opening had her eyes flying open and Liam stood there jangling a set of keys.

"Your chariot awaits, madam."

This time her stomach did a triple somersault. His face was alight with laughter and his hair had gotten mussed in the light wind. He'd loosened his tie and unbuttoned the top button of his shirt. He looked like a movie star.

"What?" Her mind was no longer focused on her trip. When he looked at her like that, she couldn't focus on anything apart from how good he looked.

"Grab your gear." A whiff of his cologne added to her bemused state as he reached across her and picked up her jacket. "It's my turn to drive you."

Liam took the keys from her and locked the truck, before he led her around to the back of the hotel. The concierge stood next to a low-slung silver Porsche and Liam handed him the ute keys, before opening the door for Georgie to climb in.

"I'll drive you to the travel agent and Queen Street.'

"Oh wow! In a Porsche, no less. Just as well I dressed up." Georgie shot him a grin. She was going to enjoy the day.

***

Georgie had been quiet when Liam had met up with her near the State Library. He'd dropped her off at her travel agency and parked the Porsche in a garage near Southbank before walking back down across the bridge. He'd filled up the hour by browsing in an antique bookstore near where he was supposed to meet her at noon. She'd been waiting on a bench on a patch of lawn near the river and had slid a blue travel wallet into her bag when he strolled across to her.

She'd looked up at him with a smile but he could have sworn her eyes were sad.

"So where to now?" he'd asked. He'd never visited Brisbane apart from the airport. Georgie had told him he was in for a treat. Since then he'd had the whole tourist experience and he'd enjoyed letting her show him the Brisbane she knew and obviously loved. She'd laughed with delight as they'd caught the River Cat down the river and back to Southbank.

They'd strolled along the waterfront through the tourist crowds, and the smell of the river surrounded them. When she'd heard that Liam had never experienced Brisbane as a tourist, she'd insisted that he hadn't lived until he'd eaten ice cream from the Southbank Ice Cream and Chocolate Shop.

As they sat outside, it seemed as if whatever had been on her mind had disappeared and she was smiling at him as he put the napkin down.

Liam grinned when the ice cream creation began to topple.

"Quick, catch it," Georgie squealed.

Now he grabbed for his spoon as the Earthquake they were sharing teetered precariously. Eight scoops of ice cream and eight different toppings including fresh bananas, whipped cream, chopped almonds, decadent chocolate chips, cherries, and more were tilting as he tried to hold them.

"Give me your spoon, too." He glanced up at

Georgie as she handed over her spoon and he placed it strategically to balance the melting ice cream. "Now what?"

"We keep eating it. I'll go get another spoon…or two." Georgie had a smudge of ice cream on her lips and he stared at it. She headed for the counter and came back with two long-handled spoons and a handful of napkins. He smoothed the pile of ice cream down and slowly lowered his two spoons as she picked up one of the others.

"You've got strawberry ice cream on your mouth." Liam reached for a napkin, dabbed at her top lip, and grinned as the colour shot into her cheeks. "Are you really going to eat all that ice cream before it melts?" They were sitting out in the courtyard in Southbank and the midday sun was warm on their heads. Georgie's sunglasses were holding her hair back from her face and she reached up, dropping them down over her eyes.

"You'll have to help me." She filled a spoon with banana and whipped cream and placed the last cherry on top before lifting it to his lips. Liam opened his mouth and she slid the spoon between his lips and stared at him, but he couldn't see the expression in her eyes.

"Your turn." Before he picked up the spoon, he lifted her sunglasses back onto her head. He wanted to see her face. Her green eyes held his as he filled the spoon with more ice cream and held it to her lips. The noise of the crowds faded around them and it was as though they were in their own private world.

Georgie licked the ice cream from the spoon and looked away as she reached for a clean napkin. "No more. I'll burst."

Liam leaned back and folded his arms waiting for his heartbeat to go back to normal. "So what have you got for me next?"

Georgie glanced at her watch. "You're not in a hurry to go home?"

Liam laughed. "After the amount I had to pay to rent the Porsche, I'm not taking it back till midnight, so you'd better find something to entertain me for another twelve hours."

Georgie's fair skin coloured and his heart skipped a beat. She was obviously thinking the same thing he was.

"We could go for a drive or we could take another cruise up the river?'

"How about we do both?" He pushed the plate with the mess of ice cream to the middle of the table and stood. Georgie picked up her bag and walked along beside him. Liam reached for her hand and smiled as her fingers curled in his.

They filled in the afternoon by walking around the wharves and taking another Rivercat cruise ride before coming back and joining the sunset cruise that went underneath the Storey Bridge. Liam laughed as she dragged him into a magnet shop in the Valley and they pored over the thousands of varieties of magnets on display.

"You're full of surprises. All the women I've ever taken shopping wanted to go to clothes and shoe stores."

She sent him a glance from beneath her long lashes. "And I suppose there were lots of women? All in the name of research, I'd guess."

It was the closest she'd gotten to asking him about his past. They'd both steered clear of personal questions.

"Hundreds," he said. He put his hand on Georgie's arm and dropped his voice. "I'd like to sit down and tell you about my…about me…one day."

"If you want," she said slowly, but she looked uneasy. He wanted to open his heart to her, to tell her about the grief and the disappointment of not being able to make his marriage work and the shock of Vanessa's death after they'd split up and how hard it had been to deal with the lies the media had told. The heaviness that had filled him until the last couple of weeks and the reason he had been so rude to her on the beach when he'd fallen from his kayak. Why he'd thought he wanted to be alone.

Liam picked up a magnet depicting a Viking

woman with long red hair holding a hammer. "This reminds me of you."

"Thanks, not." She looked at the wall in front of them and giggled and the panic faded from her expression. He wouldn't go there again.

"So if that's me, this is you." She held out a little man with a long beard hunched over a pen with a pile of books surrounding him.

After purchasing their souvenirs, Liam handed her one of the small bags as they crossed the square to the wharf where they were to pick up the cruise.

Georgie stopped walking as she took it and held his gaze steadily. "You can put yours on your desk and it will remind you of the redhead who built your bookshelves, since I'll be gone." He opened his mouth to speak, but Georgie put her fingers against his lips.

"Don't say anything. When you tell me all about you later, I'll tell you all about my trip and why I'm going away. Deal?" Her voice was soft and he reached up and held her hand against his face.

"Deal."

***

The sun set in a flash of colour as the yellow and black tourist boat cruised beneath Brisbane river bridges. The breeze had dropped and the night was still, as the sky filled with streaks of purple- and gold-edged clouds. It was one of the most amazing skies Georgie had ever seen and most of the passengers on board were all rushing to the upper deck to get a clear shot with their cameras, phones, or iPads. She stood at the side of the deck and sighed softly as a guitarist strummed his Spanish guitar from the centre of the boat. Liam was behind her with his arms loosely draped around her waist and he rested his cheek on her hair.

"Tired?"

"Mmm. A little." She leaned back against him and closed her eyes as the warmth of his body pressed into her back.

"I am. You've worn me out with your knowledge of this city." Liam's voice was quiet and his breath brushed her cheek gently as he spoke. "I've seen most of the attractions in one fell swoop. But I've had a great day."

"Me, too."

"There's only one more thing that will make it perfect."

Georgie straightened and she wondered what he was going to say. She knew what would make the day perfect, but she wasn't going to go there.

"How about we have dinner at the Ritz-Carlton at Caloundra when we take the Porsche back?" Liam smiled down at her.

"Now that *would* be a perfect end to a

wonderful day." Georgie almost jumped into his arms with excitement. "I've wanted to go there for years, but staying there is definitely out of my league. When I was a teenager I used to dream of having my wedding there in a marquee on the lawn on top of the cliff." Her face clouded as she looked away, but she kept talking. "Going back home in Ana's truck is going to be a bit of a change after driving around in that fancy car all afternoon."

###

The drive back to Caloundra was quiet. Liam closed the soft top and the luxurious car cruised the miles silently. Georgie closed her eyes and listened to the classical music coming from the stereo, trying not to think of this perfect day coming to an end. She knew when she got home that she needed to study the itinerary that Sandy had printed off for her. Her bank account was also several thousand dollars poorer, but if the truth be known, she was more excited about having dinner at the Ritz-Carlton than about her planned trip.

"Georgie?" A light touch on her arm roused her from sleep. "We're here."

She opened her eyes slowly and smoothed her hair back.

Great, I was probably drooling.

Georgie headed to the ladies' powder room off the foyer as Liam handed the Porsche keys over.

She stood in front of the huge mirror and brushed her hair until all of the tangles were gone before she swept it up into a French plait on the back of her head and secured it firmly with a clip she'd found in the bottom of her bag. Washing her face with warm water, she patted it dry with one of the soft warm towels put out for patrons' use and then reapplied her makeup. A final glance at the mirror to straighten her clothes and Georgie was satisfied she looked ready to dine in one of the most upscale restaurants on the coast. Her eyes were sparkling and there was a rosy flush on her cheeks. It wasn't from anticipation; it was a touch of the sun from today.

She looked good and she stepped into the foyer with assurance as Liam smiled appreciatively and took her arm. He'd done his shirt buttons back up and knotted his tie. She handed him his jacket and when he slipped it back on, he was the epitome of elegance.

Georgie's mouth dried. Was she really about to have dinner at the Beach Restaurant at the Ritz-Carlton with Liam Wyndham, famous author? She shook her head and Liam looked down at her.

"Is something wrong?" His voice was concerned and she loved him for it.

Oh please, don't say the L-word. Don't even think it.

"No, I was just pinching myself. This is like

a dream come true for me. Maybe I'll wake up in a minute." She shot him a grin as the maître d' led them to a table by the window, and when Georgie was seated, he flicked a snow-white napkin over her lap.

"I've been a bit presumptuous." Liam watched her as she lifted her water glass and sipped.

"Yes?" She tipped her head to the side. He had a flush on his cheeks and she wasn't sure if it was from the sun or if something was bothering him.

"I thought by the time we had dinner it would be late…and maybe we would share a bottle of wine to celebrate the end of a perfect day…"

"And?"

"And I've asked if there are any rooms available." His words came out in a rush, as though he were a nervous teen on his first date. "If you'd rather go home, we can."

Excitement coiled low in Georgie's belly, but she kept her face bland as she answered him. "Rooms or room?"

She bit back a laugh as the colour deepened beneath Liam's gorgeous cheekbones. It was usually *her* face that coloured up, and it was the first time she had seen him lose his cool.

"Ah…one room?" He held her gaze steadily, and as the waitress came over to hand them the menu, Georgie let a small smile tilt her lips.

"I think that would be a perfect end to the

day. But there's only one problem." She glanced down at her bag.

Liam frowned. "A problem?"

"I don't have any night things with me."

A huge grin spread across his face and when he winked at her, the nervous jolt shot through her whole body. "I don't think that will be a problem at all."

Chapter Seventeen

"As good as you expected?"

Liam's eyes were closed and his expression was one of pure bliss. He opened his eyes and put his fork down on his plate. "I think I can safely say that this steak is even better than that ice cream delight you made me eat for lunch."

"The purest flavours of the country for the discerning palate." Georgie read from the card on the middle of the table to keep her attention from straying to Liam's lips. They had shared a plate of plump, succulent oysters before their main course was brought to the table, and Liam had kept his eyes on her lips as he'd fed them to her. Georgie leaned the card on the ice bucket in the centre of the table before looking around the restaurant. No matter how much she was looking forward to spending the night here in *one* room, she wanted to enjoy every minute of their meal.

The restaurant was elegant and the hushed conversation of a small group across the room combined with the classical music to provide a pleasant background ambience. Georgie glanced across to the window. The lawns on the edge of the cliff were floodlit and the ocean spray was highlighted by the bright light as the waves crashed against the rocks below. She gave a little sigh of pleasure and picked up her glass. "You know, I feel like I'm in a Hollywood movie."

"So long as it's not an Alfred Hitchcock movie. Uncle Joe's house sort of reminds me of one of his thrillers." Liam nodded to the waitress as she took his plate. He looked back at Georgie and his smile faded. "So if we *were* in a movie, I guess this would be the time when the two main characters gazed into each other's eyes and talked about their past?"

Georgie hid a smile. The only restaurant movie that came to mind was that famous scene with Meg Ryan and Billy Crystal, but she sure wasn't going to mention that. Embarrassment filled her as she thought of Liam's reaction if she *were* to bring that up. Although she didn't want the happy mood of the day to disappear, if they started talking too seriously. Their surroundings were full of romance, the soft light, the low music in the background, and the private alcove they'd been seated in. It would be a perfect night for a couple in love, but she pushed that thought away. They were a long way from that.

We're simply two adults enjoying each other's company. A day spent together, a pleasant dinner in an elegant restaurant. Casual conversation followed by a night of casual… Well…that's what it was…casual sex.

Or maybe friends with benefits? That sounded better. No big deal.

Act like a grown-up, not a teenager mooning over a movie star. She fought the tremble that consumed her as she thought of the night ahead. Was she being foolish? Was she setting herself up for serious heartbreak?

"Tell me about you. What it's like to be famous?" She tried to keep her words light and Liam reached over and lifted her hand, staring at her fingers. He seemed to be searching for the right words. Finally, he broke the silence and she tried to ignore the nervous flutters running along her fingers.

"I've been happier these last couple of weeks than I have for a long time," he said softly. Liam was still staring at their joined hands. "Am I being egotistical to assume you've read some of the crap written about my life and my marriage?"

"I know you were married and your wife died while you were overseas." Georgie waited for him to look at her, and when he did, she looked back at him steadily. "The old dears devour all the gossip magazines and they hinted there was some scandal, but I didn't read it myself." She squeezed his hand. "Look, Liam. It's your business and I'm sure it was tough, but you don't have to tell me anything."

His eyes were dark as he looked back at her, and Georgie's stomach began doing double flips.

"I want to. I want you to know what you're taking on."

"Whoa." Georgie pulled her fingers from his grasp and held up her hand. "Just slow down. I'm not 'taking anything on.'" She kept her voice even, but her mind was spinning.

Too late. It was way too late. These were the words she'd yearned to hear from a man, but not now. Ahead of her was the trip where the new Georgie would find her independence. There was no longer any need for a man in her life to complete the old girlish dream.

And how foolish would I be to think that someone as gorgeous and famous as Liam would want me?

"You're kidding yourself, Liam." Her heart was thudding and Georgie took a deep breath, but the waitress came to take the rest of their order before she could finish speaking. She took the menu from the waitress and read off the first thing she could see. "Pineapple cheesecake. I might as well try the cuisine. I'll be in Hawaii soon." She stared at him as he gave the menu a cursory glance before ordering apple pie.

He waited for the waitress to leave before he spoke. Georgie's heart set up a dance beat in her chest as he looked at her. His blue eyes held hers and he reached for her hand again and she let him take it.

"Who hurt you so badly, Georgie?" His voice was husky, and his thumb caressed the back of her hand. Tears pricked the back of her eyelids but Georgie was determined not to show him that she was a quivering mess inside. Lifting her glass, she took a huge gulp of wine. She could have listed them but instead, her answer was flippant.

"We can have fun together"—she deliberately looked at him in what she hoped was a coquettish way—"and I'm looking forward to tonight. But Liam, I come from a long line of non-committers. So no involvement with *anyone* for me. Ever. I need my independence."

Huh. One of the biggest lies I've ever told.

She willed away the ache in her throat as Liam stared at her. "So we can stay friends—friends with benefits, even, but I'll be out of here in a week or two. I finalised my trip today." She put on a sexy chuckle. "And I've paid for it, so you can't even tempt me to stay. No matter how much fun we have tonight."

"I don't believe you. You sound bitter." The expression on Liam's face was doing her no good. She didn't want to talk about why she felt the way she did. "Talk to me, Georgie. I mightn't be able to help, but I am a good listener."

Not now. Not ever. But he kept looking at her, waiting for her to answer and she heaved a small sigh.

"There's nothing to talk about. The bottom line is, I've decided to take off and see the world." Georgie swallowed and tried to make her words dismissive as she lifted her hand from his. "It's time for adventure and there's nothing for me here anymore…" No matter how long she had waited for a man like him, it still didn't feel real. She would give in and then he wouldn't want her the way she wanted him. It always happened, and this time she would not be the one falling first.

***

The glib exterior that Georgie was hiding behind didn't fool Liam for one minute, and he could sense she was trying to cover up something. What it was, he couldn't pinpoint exactly. The day had been fun, and he'd been looking forward to the night ahead. He hadn't told her, but he'd booked the suite overlooking the ocean.

Maybe it's not the right time?

They ate their desserts quietly, the soft music filling the silence between them. Liam raised the wine bottle and waited for Georgie to look at him. She'd spent a lot of time with her head turned to the window, watching the spray of the ocean dancing in the spotlight outside the restaurant.

"More wine?"

"No, thank you." Her lips tilted in a smile and

the rush that tore through him almost took his breath away. "I couldn't eat or drink another thing. It was beautiful. Thank you for bringing me here."

Liam reached across and took her hand. "You're beautiful." The feeling that filled his chest when her fingers curled in his was like nothing he'd ever experienced before.

Maybe he should pull back now, or it was going to be very hard for him when she went away. And she seemed determined to go. When she'd said there was nothing left for her in Maleny, her eyes had been sad. He'd seen her with her friends at his welcome party and he knew that it wasn't true. She was loved by everyone there that afternoon, but now there was hesitancy in her expression that showed him that she didn't realise how important she was to those people. There had been so much hurt in her voice, even though she'd tried to cover it. All he wanted to do was to take her in his arms and make everything better for her. He looked down at her small hand entwined in his and brushed his thumb over the soft skin. She looked up at him and her eyes were dark.

Should they go home to their respective houses? Was he taking advantage of her vulnerability?

Georgie pulled her hand from his and rose, pushing her chair back. "I don't know about you, but

I'm tired. It's been a busy day."

Liam cleared his throat. "So?"

"So take me upstairs and show me...show me this wonderful room you've booked."

"You're sure?"

Georgie smiled and nodded.

Liam called for the bill and signed the check and tipped the waitress while Georgie waited by the window, watching the waves smash against the rocks. He walked over and slipped his arm around her waist and closed his eyes as she leaned back against his chest.

"I love the water. Whenever I'm upset, I walk on the beach and watch the waves and it soothes me here." She raised her hand to her chest and Liam placed his hand against hers, brushing against the softness of her breast.

Georgie drew a quick breath and Liam dropped his head, brushing his lips against her cheek.

"Come on, I've already picked up our room key."

They walked together to the elevator, and anticipation curled in Liam's belly as they waited for the door to open. He stood back and waited for an older couple to enter before them, when all he wanted to do was rush in there and get to their room. Georgie stared back at him as the elevator rose quietly and smoothly to the top floor.

"Have a good evening." The elderly gentleman nodded at them as they walked along the hall, and Liam could have sworn he had a gleam in his eye.

Surprised to feel his hands trembling as he swiped the room key, he pushed the door open.

"Oh. My. Goodness." Georgie's voice was hushed as she stood beside him and looked around. "The ocean suite?"

Liam nodded, feeling like a teenager on his first date. His mouth was dry and his breath caught as he watched Georgie hold her arms wide and spin in a circle.

Fighting back the need that was pulsing through him, Liam followed her across to the window and stood beside her as they took in the majesty of the rolling swells pushing into the cliffs. Finally Georgie turned and splayed her hands on his chest. He was sure she could feel his heart thudding beneath his shirt.

"The view is amazing. Thank you for booking the suite," she whispered. "Are you sure you can afford this?"

"At least you've stopped saying sorry all the time." He grinned at her as her eyes widened, and he was touched by her concern. "And yes, I can afford it."

Liam moved slowly, watching Georgie's

green eyes as he took her face between his hands and dipped his head to taste her. Her breath sighed out through sweet lips and her eyes closed as he felt her hands move from his chest to grip the top of his arms. His legs were unsteady as a surge of panic rushed through him.

I love this woman. Certainty filled him. Liam was as sure of that as he was that the sun would rise in the morning. He didn't want to. He wasn't ready to go anywhere near there, and besides, she was leaving.

Never again, he'd vowed when his marriage had died.

But the feelings that coursed through him were new and unfamiliar. Liam closed his eyes and gave in to them. He needed to think it through, but with Georgie's fingers loosening his tie and moving to the buttons of his shirt, he was captivated, and his confused thoughts disappeared as Georgie pushed the shirt from his shoulders and her warm hands settled on his bare chest.

Chapter Eighteen

"So what's for breakfast?"

Liam opened his eyes slowly. Georgie was sitting in the chair by the window, looking out over the glistening water. It was like a millpond this morning; the long lazy swells of the Pacific Ocean had settled to a calm surface and there was no sound of waves crashing below them. She'd obviously showered; her hair was damp and she was dressed in her clothes from yesterday.

"Me?" he asked hopefully.

Georgie laughed and pointed to the clock beside the bed. "I've got work to do. A certain author is in need of some bookshelves, and I also suspect he may have some writing to do." She tipped her head to the side and Liam reluctantly pushed himself up against the soft pillows at the head of the bed.

"True. We do need to get back to work. Or at least I do." He held her gaze steadily. "I'm really impressed with my builder's...er...skills and it wouldn't worry me if she took a year or so to finish the job."

Georgie was the first to break eye contact.

"But yes, breakfast downstairs first. I've noticed how much you love your food. And then we'll find your old ute." Liam swung his legs over the side of the bed.

Georgie's hand flew to her mouth. "Oh, no."

"What's wrong?" For a moment Liam thought he'd said the wrong thing about her enjoying food. Maybe she was like Vanessa, who'd thought it was not feminine to enjoy eating, but he didn't think so. Especially not after that Earthquake ice cream she'd devoured yesterday.

"Your new car," she exclaimed. "You were going to go to the car dealership yesterday but I dragged you around the tourist traps and we totally forgot all about it."

Liam shook his head. "I didn't." His kept his voice rather smug. "I ordered one when you were at the travel agency."

"Ordered one? Without even taking it for a test drive?" Georgie wrinkled her nose and a surge of warmth shot through him. Her face was full of joy and he enjoyed being with her. Last night had been magic and he'd woken a few times through the night and just enjoyed feeling her pressed against him, breathing softly as she slept. He'd run his fingers gently through her hair and she'd stirred slightly but hadn't woken.

He'd pushed away the doubts that niggled at the edge of his mind. He'd think it through when they got home. Or rather when he was home at his house.

"We did take a test drive."

"What?" Confusion was written all over her face. "When?"

"The Porsche," he said. "I ordered one. All I had to do was pick the colour and I went for the silver. They're trucking a new one up from Sydney later this week. I'll pick it up here."

"Oh, wow. You won't want to get in the old noisy truck with me anymore, will you?" Georgie grinned at him as she stood and crossed to the door. "I'll go down and wait in the breakfast room while you shower and dress. Okay?"

***

Georgie sat beside the window in the restaurant and stared out over the water. The morning sunlight glistened on the breaking waves and the soft shush of the surf echoed her pensive mood. After Liam had gone to sleep in the early hours, she had lain there beside him. His hand had been resting on her hip and she'd closed her eyes and listened to his breathing. A smidgeon of hope had slowly filled her in the still of the dawn, and she began to think that maybe this time, just maybe, things might be different.

Yesterday had been perfect. The only downside had been spending the time and her money at the travel agency. For a brief moment last night, Georgie had wondered what would happen if she just put the trip on hold for a while and hung around.

237

Hung around Liam and waited to see what developed.

No. She was going on her trip; she was not going to leave herself open to more hurt.

"Coffee, madam?"

She smiled up at the waiter as he held the coffee pot up. "Black, please." He filled her cup and stepped away and Georgie's breath caught in her throat, all her conviction fading. Liam stood in the doorway looking around the tables and she fought for composure as his eyes settled on her. His hair was damp, and he hadn't shaved. She smiled as she watched him cross the room to her.

To me. All the women in the room turned and watched as he walked past their tables. Georgie knew Liam was totally unaware of how sexy he was, and that just added to his attraction.

And she had spent the night in his bed. A little bud of warmth unfurled in her chest.

Maybe?

***

Liam pulled the chair out and sat opposite Georgie. "I'm starving."

As she lifted her eyes to meet his, a smile lit up her face and an unfamiliar rush of need flooded through him.

"You've worn me out, woman. I need food." He tried to cover up his confusion by being flippant.

"Good, it will give you energy to write all day."

"I can think of better ways to spend the day." Liam reached out and took her hand, but Georgie shook her head.

"I have work to do, and so do you."

Liam looked down at her fingers laced with his. "Georgie?"

"Yes?" She tipped her head to the side.

"Would you consider putting your trip off for a while?"

"Why? So I can do the second room of shelves for you?" A frown crossed her face and Liam held her fingers more firmly.

"No, of course not. I don't care about the shelves. I mean, I do. I want them, and you are doing a great job, but that's not what I meant." Liam stared at her and her green eyes widened. "I mean let's spend some more time together. Can you change your itinerary?"

"No." Georgie stared back at him but it was hard to read her expression. He was hoping that he would be able to tempt her to stay.

"I'm doing a favour for a friend in Hawaii over Christmas." She pulled her hand back from his and rested her elbows on the table, with her chin cupped in her hand.

Before he could reply, the waiter appeared

with the menu and their conversation turned to food.

***

On the way back up the Bruce Highway, Georgie was grateful for the rattling of the old ute. Liam seemed to be in a world of his own and stared through the window as the coast flashed past them.

Her independence was taking flight. It seemed to have a mind of its own. She needed to get that new mantra tattooed on her arm to stop her from staying here—for a guy.

I value my independence. What the heck had she been thinking of to spend the day—and the night—with him? She was falling in love with Liam, and who was going to get hurt? Just like every other time—her. Georgie straightened her shoulders and gripped the steering wheel harder as they approached the shared driveway to their houses. The sooner she got away from him, the better.

She forced a grin onto her face as she turned up to his house. "I'll drop you off and then I'm going to take Mutt for a walk." Hopefully, she could keep some of her dignity intact. "Thank you for last night. It was very pleasant."

Liam shot her a glance and opened his door. "I'll see you later, then."

"Yes, you will." She kept the bright smile on her face until she backed down the drive and turned into the gate of Cliff Cottage.

***

Very pleasant?

God, that was as bad as her telling him she'd had a nice time. Liam pushed the front door open and strode across the tiled foyer. He was falling for Georgie and should really pull back. It had been a magical night together, but she'd soon be gone. He shrugged as he headed for the study. Immerse himself in Nepal; that was the solution. He had a hero to sort out today. He'd cope once she was gone. He'd have to. Once she left, he would settle into his novels and his house and he'd forget about her. Liam tried to push away the thought of Georgie sleeping in his arms, but it wouldn't go. All he could see was her lustrous auburn hair splayed across his chest as she'd lain beside him.

What the hell was he thinking? No more pondering emotions or red-haired beauties. Liam shrugged off his suit jacket and switched on his computer. He'd get changed later, when he broke for a coffee. The computer whirred to life and he accessed the cloud drive where he'd last saved his work. As he scrolled through the last chapters he'd written, Georgie's face stayed with him. Then the feelings that had consumed him for the past twenty-four hours turned into letters and words and his fingers flew over the keyboard. But he wasn't going to hold her back. He pulled a face as he typed. This time the tables were turned. For once, he was the needy person, but he couldn't keep Georgie from doing what she wanted. If she didn't go on this trip, because he asked her to stay, she'd end up resenting him later. It would be like Vanessa all over again.

In a way, it was like a purging. Liam knew he couldn't afford to trust his heart, no matter what he thought he felt for Georgie. He'd learned that the hard way.

God, even the name of this book is *Guardian of the Village*. It didn't matter that his hero was high up in the lofty Himalayas. His own heart was in just as much jeopardy here in Hideaway Bay.

He'd be guarding it until she left on her trip, that's for sure.

Liam stood and frowned at his watch as the sound of a door closing caught his attention. He stretched, surprised to see how long he'd been at the computer. It was mid-afternoon. Georgie was late starting work. He'd managed to operate on two levels while he'd worked. The story had flowed and he was more than satisfied with its progress. But he was less than satisfied with the emotions that ran through him. No matter how hard he tried, he couldn't shift them.

Georgie was firmly embedded in his head, but he'd just have to get used to the idea of her leaving, though he couldn't understand why she was so set on moving away. She was as much a part of this community as the cliffs along the beach. He was sure she wasn't being true to herself. But Liam had already experienced enough dishonesty with Vanessa.

Whatever happened with Georgie, however he felt, whatever she thought, he was going to be honest. Before he went upstairs to the study, he switched on the coffeemaker and went to get changed into his jeans. Liam tipped his head to the side and listened as he headed back to the kitchen. It was completely quiet, apart from the burbling of the coffee machine and the noise of the waves breaking on the rocks at the bottom of the cliff. There was no sound coming from above.

Shrugging, he poured two coffees and headed up the stairs, prepared to be completely honest with Georgie. If she blew him off, so be it. Balancing the coffee cups in one hand, he pushed open the door and looked around the room. The room was empty. The closing door that had disturbed him must have been her leaving.

He'd do some more writing and then he'd go down to the cottage to see her.

Maybe.

Chapter Nineteen

Georgie was being a coward. As soon as she finished the trim on the middle shelf, she packed up quietly and then jumped into the ute. She headed for Thelma and Mitzi's house, even though it was only mid-afternoon. The more time she spent away from Liam the better. No more nights together. She'd focus on his bookshelves, get them finished, and get ready for her trip. Time to ease back before it was too hard to leave and she couldn't. They were good together and they'd had fun, but she was leaving and he wasn't going to entice her to stay.

"Georgie! We haven't seen you for ages."

She shot a dry smile at Thelma. "All of three days. I was here on Sunday, remember?"

"But you've been busy with your young man. So we quite understand if you're too busy to call on us, don't we, Mitzi?"

"You two are incorrigible!" Georgie couldn't help the laugh that escaped as she hugged Thelma. "I'm here now, so what's for dinner?"

Conversation was lively as she sat in the kitchen and watched her friends whip up a meal.

"It's a shame you didn't bring Liam with you." Thelma looked sideways at Mitzi as she stirred the pot of soup she'd taken from the refrigerator.

"I know what the pair of you are up to." Georgie forced a smile on her face but shook her head. "It's not going to happen. I'm leaving in less than two weeks."

Two wrinkled faces fell with a collective sigh. Thelma pulled out a chair and sat beside her. "We so hoped that you and Liam would get together. It would have been a perfect ending. Things would have come full circle for us."

"What do you mean?"

Mitzi put the spoon on to the sink and came to sit at the table. "Because of Joe." Her voice was soft. "Liam's Uncle Joe and I were dating. He used to drive me around in the Fireflite. And then he went to Vietnam." She wiped a tear away and Georgie reached out to her and held her soft hand. "I waited for him to come back, but I was foolish. He was the love of my life and I didn't tell him before he went away. When he came back, he had a wife." Georgie squeezed Mitzi's fingers as her voice wavered. "I left it too late. Don't you dare make the same mistake."

Thelma chimed in. "We thought it would be perfect, if you, part of our family, and Liam got together and closed the circle."

Georgie shook her head. "Oh, you sweet things. I'm sorry, but it's not going to happen. Liam doesn't need me in his life. He's a famous author. He has his career, and besides, it wasn't that long ago that his wife died."

She stared at the two expectant faces across

the table. "And I'm about to leave on my big adventure. I can't fall in love just because you want me to." She kept her voice steady and the smile on her face. There was no way anyone would ever know she *had* fallen in love with the man. Not even Sienna. It was her secret and if she was going to get over him and leave…no one else was going to know how she felt. No more wearing her heart on her sleeve.

Yes, she'd finally admitted it to herself. She had fallen in love…again. But no, it wasn't again. This was the first time in her life she had experienced this feeling. All the other times she'd just thought it was love. Now she knew the difference. Even more reason for not taking the risk of being the one left behind. It had hurt her ego the other times; if Liam knew how she felt and left her, this time her heart would be shattered.

"I'm off to see the world, and I promise I'll send you a postcard from every stop I make. Now is that soup almost done? I'm starving."

Yes, I carried that off perfectly. All she had to do was keep it together until she left. Be jolly, happy Georgie, and get her bags packed. She could cry as much as she liked on her way to Hawaii.

***

For the first time since he'd moved into the house on the cliff, Liam regretted not having a car at his disposal. The cottage below sat in darkness. It would have been good to have jumped in a car and gone for a drive along the coast. He was pleased he'd be able to pick his Porsche up next week. As he thought of going up to the city, he realised he hadn't called Sarah about the cancelled meeting with the editor.

He went in search of his mobile and found it on the floor beside his computer. He had been altogether too vague since he'd met Georgie, but at least he'd been back in his creative zone. Having a break from both tonight might be good.

"Sarah?" His agent picked up straightaway. "It's me, Liam."

"Good to hear from you. I was going to call you tomorrow." Her voice was wary. "So how did the meeting with the editor go? I've been waiting for you to call."

"Sorry. I've been…a bit busy. Larissa didn't show—her flight was cancelled. She's rescheduled for next week." Liam wandered over to the window and looked down the hill. Still no lights on at the cottage.

"So are we."

"We?"

"Mike and me." Sarah spoke quickly. "We're staying at the Fairmont in Caloundra. Look, we're just out for dinner. I'll call later and we'll organise a time to meet up. I'll come to the meeting with you."

"Great." Liam meant it. It would be good to catch up with his friends. "Oh. And Sarah?" He tried not to sound too smug. "First ten chapters are finished and I've got another book to show her, too. A short one."

But the first thing he was going to do was sort out his feelings for Georgie. He knew he couldn't fight them any longer. For the first time in many months, Liam was happy. Happy where he was and with what he was doing. The one thing to complete his happiness would be to have Georgie by his side. All he had to do was convince her of that. He'd give her time to miss him, and he'd put the days to good use. One thing about falling in love: his muse was back with a vengeance.

***

The days passed quickly for Georgie. She was up early each morning, worked all day, and was home in the early afternoon. She went out every afternoon and stayed out for dinner, catching up with her friends and saying good-bye. Thelma and Mitzi wanted to put on a farewell party for her but she refused, trying to be gentle when she saw their disappointment.

Liam had stayed in his study each day, and Georgie wondered why he was avoiding her. Hopefully, he'd decided to move on and that the couple of nights they had spent together were just a casual…casual what? She couldn't face another night with him and then leave. She was barely keeping it together now. Putting on such a brave "happy Georgie" front with her friends was taking its toll. But despite being so tired, sleep was a long time coming each night.

She decided to work all weekend and was putting the last trim on the bookshelf along the far wall on Sunday afternoon when there was a tap on the door. She jumped down from the stepladder and smoothed her hair back as she crossed the room, schooling her expression into a friendly smile.

The numbness of the last few days deepened when she opened the door. She had put her feelings on ice. Liam leaned against the doorjamb and looked at her, casual and…well…just gorgeous. His signature white shirt was unbuttoned, but he wore a white T-shirt beneath. Fighting to keep a friendly and welcoming expression— tradesperson to client—on her face, Georgie tucked the hammer into her work belt.

"Hi, stranger. You've been busy writing?"

He looked at her and those sexy blue eyes didn't blink. Goose bumps prickled Georgie's skin from her neck all the way down her arms. Her fingers shook, and she ran her hands up and down her arms briskly.

"Gosh, that breeze is strong coming down the

corridor." She turned away from him and walked over to the open window and pulled it down. Her back was to him and she closed her eyes. "Could you close the door, please?"

Keep calm, stop babbling. Play it cool.

Slow footsteps followed her across the room, and she opened her eyes and picked up a handful of nails. "Do you mind if I keep working?"

Liam still hadn't spoken a word.

Georgie placed one nail at the edge of the fancy trim and pulled the hammer from her belt. "Shelves are looking good. I hope you're happy with them." She felt him behind her before his breath brushed the back of her bare neck. Her hair was twisted in a high ponytail. "How is the book coming along?" God, the cheeriness in her voice sounded false even to her.

"Would you have dinner with me tonight?" Liam's voice was soft and his mouth must have been awfully close, because his breath now warmed her ear.

Yes, oh yes. No, I can't. Oh God, help me.

"Ah, I'm not sure what my plans are." She put another nail between her lips and dug into her belt for a couple more, feeling very clever. Even if he wanted to kiss her, he couldn't.

Gentle hands reached across; one took the hammer from her grasp, and the other slid slowly to her waist and turned her around. She looked up at him, the cold nail pressing into her lip. Liam's eyes were dancing with mirth, and he reached up and took it from between her lips.

"If you think that is going to stop you from talking to me, you're wrong." He led her across to the wide windowsill and gently pushed her down until she was looking up at him. He put the hammer on the floor before he leaned over in front of her, one hand on each side of her on the windowsill. "I've given you a few days to work in peace, although it's been hard to stay away."

The look on Liam's face almost broke her determination to resist him, and she swallowed before she opened her mouth, but he shook his head. "I want *you* to listen to me. Don't talk."

Her skin was tight, and all Georgie wanted was to feel Liam stroking her skin, holding her. Her traitorous body was clamouring for him. His hands were still beside her and his face was a whisper away, but he didn't touch her. Her heart panicked in her chest as the ice began to crack.

No.

"You are beautiful, Georgie." When she screwed up her nose in dissent, Liam shook his head. "And I mean inside and out. Your lovely hair, your milk-white skin. Green witch eyes that see into my soul; eyes that I know understand me. A mouth that tempts me"—he smiled and she trembled—"even with nails in it."

The ice around her heart cracked a little more. Georgie swore she could feel the warmth spreading through her chest. His lips hovered above hers but did not come closer.

"You are caring, patient, and sweet, and you give so much of yourself to others."

The warmth of his skin surrounded her but still he didn't touch her.

"In your smile, I see someone so gorgeous, and when you smile at me"—finally he lifted his hand, but he put it on his heart—"this is where I feel it."

Cautious optimism fluttered through her. Almost…almost…she could believe he meant what he was saying to her. She leaned into him.

"One word." His voice was deep and mellow, and his expression was dreamy as he held her gaze.

Oh my God, if he used the L-word, Georgie knew she'd melt into a puddle at his feet. She widened her eyes and waited.

"Yes…just say yes." His breath brushed her lips.

Georgie's voice shook. "I don't know what the question is."

"Spend the night with me? I'll cook dinner and then we'll talk some more. Okay?" Liam stepped back and Georgie nodded before she managed to croak out a yes. He turned quickly and threw a smiling glance back at her when he reached the door.

"Seven o'clock, okay?"

She nodded again, feeling like one of those dolls with the bobbing head.

"And Georgie, wear that green dress you had on the other day. I'll put the fire on."

The door closed behind him and Georgie put her hands to her cheeks. She wouldn't need a fire. The blood pumping through her body would be enough to keep both of them warm.

Mutt started howling as Georgie closed the gate behind her. Having time to think this afternoon had not been good. The way Liam had looked at her and the words he had spoken had planted a tiny seed of hope within her. Her distrust began to lift, and she'd smiled at herself in Ana's mirror as she'd taken extra care with her appearance. A little kernel of an idea began to take shape in her head. He'd asked her to put her trip off a while, but maybe he could come with her?

She pulled her shawl around her shoulders as she walked slowly up the hill, and the wind caught the green dress Liam had asked her to wear, pushing it against her legs. The temperature had dropped; a storm was brewing over the sea. Her heart fluttered a little as she stood outside his door, and she chastised herself. This was crazy. She'd walked through this door every day for the past three weeks. There was no need to feel nervous.

The door opened before she could knock.

"Quick, come in out of that wind." Liam looked up at the threatening sky and then down at her dress. He grinned and ushered her inside, a gentle hand on her back. "I've just got to check on something in the kitchen." He cocked his head to the side. "Is that Mutt I hear?"

Georgie relaxed a little as she looked up at him. He was babbling as much as she did when she was nervous. She tipped her head to the side. "No, just the wind. He's safely inside the cottage."

They sat in front of the fire while they ate, and Liam kept the conversation casual. Finally, after he'd brought in a tray with coffee and chocolates, he slid over next to her and took her hand.

"So?" he said.

"So, what?" Georgie reached for her coffee. She'd managed to talk normally through the meal, and tried not to appear too nervous although every time she caught Liam looking at her a fresh tremble would run down her back.

"So did you think about what I said this afternoon?"

"Y…e…s," she said slowly.

"And?"

"And what?"

"Oh, for goodness' sake, Georgie, you are the most frustrating woman." He put his hand to his heart and grinned at her. Her heart rate kicked up a notch. It was altogether unfair that a man could be so good-looking.

She shook her head. "Liam, I don't know what you want from me. What you said this afternoon was really sweet, but you've forgotten I'm leaving."

Liam took the coffee cup from her hand. "No, I haven't. I wouldn't ask you not to go. I'd never do that."

His blue eyes held hers, and Georgie's determination to make her own way in the world slipped a little more. "I've got a better idea." Georgie swallowed and stared back at him. "Why don't you come with me?"

Liam shook his head slowly. "Thanks, but I'm not going anywhere. I just got here and besides…"

"Besides what?"

"I like being settled. My days of travel are over."

"And mine are just beginning." Even though Georgie's smile was bright, Liam's words cut deep, but there was no way she was going to let him see how much he hurt her. They could have time together before she left, and she would stay strong. No man was ever going to see how vulnerable she was. Never again.

"I'll send you a postcard so you can see what you're missing out on." Georgie stared at Liam and held out her hand. "I'm cold. I think we'll be warmer in your bedroom?" She was proud of the coquettish smile she managed to summon up, hiding the hurt that had settled in her chest at his instant refusal of her suggestion to come with her.

Three hours later, Georgie stood at the window of Liam's bedroom looking out over the ocean. The storm had blown itself out, not that they had heard much of it… Liam had whispered sweet nothings in her ear before taking her to delightful places. Now the night sky was filled with stars, and the silver sheen from the rising moon polished the ocean. Hugging her arms around herself, Georgie stared out at the water. It was going to be so hard to leave, but she was going to. When Liam had dismissed her suggestion that he go with her, her world had fallen to pieces, but she'd been strong and hidden her feelings. She was leaving.

It was still ten days until she left and she would spend the time with Liam. Maybe when she was old and grey like Thelma and Mitzi, it would be a story to tell. Georgie smiled and walked across the soft carpet back to the bed where Liam lay sleeping.

Chapter Twenty

Georgie tooted the horn of the old ute and glanced down at her watch. If Liam didn't hurry up, he'd miss his appointment. He was meeting his new editor in Brisbane and then picking up his new Porsche. She was going to the city for some final shopping before she packed.

She looked up with a smile as Liam came out of the house and slammed the door. He was wearing a pale grey suit and a white shirt with his hair loose on his collar. God, she was going to miss him. Georgie swallowed and dug deep for strength.

He looked down at the suit with a grin as he put an envelope on the seat between them. "Second time in two weeks I've had my suit out, but I have to impress the new editor."

"And you'll sure look the part in the new car." Georgie loved to tease him. Sometimes she wondered if she was making the wrong decision, and then she remembered her mantra.

Independence.

The traffic on the motorway was heavy, and they were late getting into the city.

"Just drop me off at the hotel." Liam leaned over and kissed her before he opened the door. "I'll take you for a spin in the Porsche this afternoon."

"I'll look forward to it—*after* I get some

work done on your shelves. Have a good meeting."

Liam waited on the kerb until she drove off, and Georgie sighed as she glanced in the rear view mirror and saw him standing there watching her. It was getting harder by the day; the more time they spent together, the harder it was going to be to leave him. Georgie waited for the light to change and frowned as she looked down at the seat. Shoot. Liam had had left his envelope on the seat. As soon as the light changed, she did a U-turn and headed back to the hotel. She pulled into the drop-off area beneath the ornate grey arches and jumped out.

"I'll only be one minute." The concierge nodded and she grabbed the envelope and ran across to the door. Luckily, she'd dressed for a trip to the city and didn't feel out of place in the luxurious foyer. Georgie's heels clicked on the marble floor as she crossed toward the main desk along the wall and looked around. Her professional eye appreciated the marble columns rising to the fancy gilded ceiling.

Liam was standing by the elevator door and Georgie opened her mouth to call out to him, but the sound died in her throat as he held his arms out to an elegant blonde woman who stepped from the elevator. Liam had told her he'd never even met the editor his publisher had sent to Brisbane.

Georgie took a shuddering breath as pain sliced through her. The woman he was holding had her hands on either side of his face and he was smiling down at her, his face alight. It was the same way he'd looked at Georgie only hours ago. As she watched, he lowered his head and the woman lifted her face to his as she slid her arms around him. Georgie turned and ran, unable to watch for a second longer. It felt as though the breath had left her chest and her heart was surrounded by ice. She pushed her way through a crowd of people coming through the door, not caring as she forced her way through. A roaring sound filled her ears and she jumped into the truck and tried to turn the key, but her hands were shaking too much. Georgie took a deep breath and wiped away the tears that were filling her eyes, making it impossible to see clearly. Taking a deep breath, she forced her hand to stop shaking long enough to start the truck.

She drove into the traffic not knowing where she was going, trying to force away the feeling that she was going to throw up.

It had happened again, but this time her heart was in tatters. She had ever experienced the heart-wrenching grief that consumed her. It was a physical pain, and she didn't know how to make it go away.

***

Georgie had managed to get a couple of hours' sleep. Now Thelma and Mitzi comforted her with shoulder pats and hugs as she'd sat at their

260

kitchen table drinking coffee. After going back to Ana's house and packing up as quickly as she could, Georgie had called in at Uncle Renzo's house and dropped off Mutt and Sooky, but she needed a female shoulder—or two—to cry on. Ana's ute was now parked in the garage next to the Fireflite and Aldo was picking her up shortly and taking her to Brisbane in his taxi.

For no fare, of course. Even the thought of his kindness brought a fresh wave of tears to Georgie's eyes and started Thelma and Mitzi fussing over her again. Her gaze fell on a pile of magazines on the table and before Mitzi could move it away, she spotted Liam's face on the front cover.

"I should have known what I was letting myself in for, right?" She sniffed and pushed the magazine away. At least the woman in the photo with him wasn't the one she'd seen in the hotel. Of course not; he was famous. Someone that famous would have a woman in every city. Georgie knew she was being unfair, but she'd seen him with her own eyes. The enormity of what she'd seen, and more importantly, of how gullible she'd been to trust him, settled like a chill in her body. The terrible picture of Liam about to kiss that woman would not leave her mind.

Mitzi wrung her hands as she stared at Georgie, her eyes filling with tears. "I can't believe it, Georgie. I saw the way Liam looked at you."

Georgie shook her head. "I saw him with my own eyes." Her phone beeped, and she picked it up and read the message.

Will see you at the airport. Love Sienna and Jack xxx

Georgie's eyes filled again. Of course Thelma and Mitzi had rung Sienna when she'd turned up yesterday afternoon looking for somewhere to spend the night. She'd spent an hour crying on the phone to Sienna. The whole world probably knew by now what a gullible fool she was.

A gullible, unlovable fool. With no chance of ever being part of a couple. She just didn't have it in her. No wonder Liam hadn't wanted to come to Hawaii with her.

Thelma passed Georgie the box of tissues as she sniffed again.

Chapter Twenty-One

Liam was late getting back to the coast. He'd tried to call Georgie to tell her he'd been delayed because the car delivery had been delayed, and then the traffic had been heavy due to an accident on the motorway, but she hadn't picked up. It was dark by the time he pulled into the old garage at his house where the pink Fireflite had resided for many years. He looked down the hill but the cottage was dark. Georgie must have gone visiting again. Liam was looking forward to becoming a part of this community and a part of her life. He'd invited Sarah and Mike down tomorrow. He couldn't wait for them to meet Georgie and see his new place.

"You look amazing." When Sarah had finally stopped hugging him, she'd stepped back and looked him up and down with a smile. "In fact, you look too good, Liam. Where has the suffering writer look gone?" Later, when he told her he'd met someone, Sarah had smiled.

The meeting with Larissa, the new editor, had gone well. They'd all laughed when he realised he'd forgotten his manuscript.

"Damn. I've left my notes and my flash drive in Georgie's car." Luckily, Larissa had been happy with the chapters he'd emailed earlier, and when they'd finished discussing business, Sarah had called up to their room and Mike had come back down and joined them for a quick drink.

Liam waited up for Georgie till almost midnight before he went to bed. She must have decided to stay down at the cottage rather than disturb him. It would be the first night in a week they had been apart, and he went to bed disappointed that she hadn't called.

****

He slept soundly and headed down the hill to the cottage first thing. He wanted to make sure Georgie would be around to meet Mike and Sarah after lunch.

The gate to the road was padlocked and Liam frowned as he stared at the house. There was no sign of the old ute or Mutt, and the house blinds were all drawn. Liam strode across the lawn and ran up the steps. The house was locked up, but he still knocked on the door as an uneasy feeling overtook him. The place looked as though it had been closed up. Georgie had never closed the blinds or locked the gate the whole time he'd lived up the hill.

He hurried back up the hill, pleased he'd grabbed the keys to his new car before he'd headed out. Liam jumped in and drove to Maleny, keeping an eye out for the old ute, but there was no sign of it at the hardware store or parked in the main street. Frowning, he turned onto the road that led down to

Thelma and Mitzi's cottage. *Maybe Georgie had gone to visit and stayed there for the night?*

As soon as he turned into the driveway he knew something was not right. The two elderly ladies were sitting on their front porch. Mitzi was dabbing at her eyes with a lace-edged handkerchief. Thelma rose slowly to her feet, her arms folded. There was not a welcoming smile to be seen.

"Liam." Thelma nodded and Mitzi blew her nose. "Why are you here?" Thelma gestured for her sister to sit back down as Mitzi rose shakily to her feet.

"I'm looking for Georgie. Have you seen her?"

"Why?"

"There's somebody I want her to meet."

"*Hmm*. Is there?" Thelma's voice was cold and Liam scratched his head.

"So do you know where she is?"

Mitzi grabbed Thelma's arm and her voice was soft. "Tell him, Thel."

"She's at the airport. The poor darling was so upset, she decided to leave early."

"Upset?" Liamlooked from one to the other. "Why was she upset? What happened?"

"See, I told you." Mitzi stood up this time and walked across to the step to stand beside Liam. "I knew it couldn't be true. I tried to tell her that."

Thelma's voice was low and she frowned at her sister. "So why were you in a clinch with a woman you'd never met when Georgie went back to the hotel to give you your manuscript?"

Suddenly it was blindingly obvious what had happened. Liam swore and Mitzi gasped.

Of all the things to happen.

***

Liam drove back to the coast and as far as the lookout. He parked the car and stared out over the ocean, his thoughts swirling through his head. Georgie's seeing him hugging Sarah had set off a chain of events that may have saved him from making a terrible mistake—the same one he'd made before. Vanessa had been needy, and he'd sworn he would never get caught by a needy woman again. He'd thought he'd fallen for Georgie, and she'd fought him every step of the way, but like the soft-hearted romantic he was, he hadn't listened. Now Liam forced himself to step back and think about what he had really wanted when he came here to Hideaway Bay. What he'd wanted and where he'd ended up.

Where he wanted to be.

Find the muse. Write my books. Okay, that was done and he was happy.

Have my privacy. Be a recluse like Uncle Joe had been. He hadn't had that. A red-haired carpenter had breached his privacy as soon as he'd arrived. And she'd introduced him to the community and to her family. *And I loved every minute of it.*

Never travel again. The horror that had filled him when he had been in Nepal and heard of Vanessa's death had firmed his resolve to settle and never travel overseas again. Liam knew that fear was irrational, but it had been real to him. He'd almost burned his passport.

Spend my days alone writing. Liam thought of the nights Georgie had spent in his bed, how she'd shown him the sights of Brisbane. The joy on her face as she'd chased the dog on the beach, the little wrinkle on her forehead when she was measuring his bookshelves. The feeling that filled him when he held her in his arms.

Liam didn't want to be alone. Knowing he'd hurt Georgie, even if unintentionally, was worse than any of his other fears.

Never have anyone need him again. Georgie was vulnerable, and he knew she'd been hurt even though she hadn't told him.

Liam opened the car door and climbed out of the car. He stood looking out to the bay as he came to a decision.

He hadn't been able to give Vanessa what she'd wanted, and he knew now it was because he'd never loved her. When he'd arrived in Hideaway Bay he'd been closed down, and what he'd believed had been right for him had been turned around by a green-eyed, red-haired woman who had bewitched him.

He loved Georgie Sacchi and he was not going to let her go.

No matter what it took.

Chapter Twenty-Two

Georgie walked toward the coffee shop at Brisbane International Airport where she'd arranged to meet Sienna and Jack. Her head was bowed and she lugged her carry-on bag over her shoulder, not watching where she was going. She barrelled straight into the tall man standing in front of her.

"Sorry," she muttered and stepped to the side to go around him. When he moved to block her way, Georgie looked up and she gasped. Blue eyes stared down at her and his lips lifted in a smile. She almost smiled back before reality hit her.

Liam? Here?

"What the hell are you doing here?" She looked around, desperate to get away from him before she made a fool of herself.

Liam took her arm and she tried to shake it off.

"Let me through, please." She tried to keep her voice cold and not look at him. As she looked down she saw the bag on the floor next to him. Lifting her head, she frowned at him. "Where are you going?"

"Hawaii." A tender smile curved his lips "If you'll let me come with you."

"What?" she said stupidly. "Why would you

want to come with me? You said you've had enough adventures."

"Because I love you?" He took the bag off her shoulder as he looked down at her. "And because I can sit next to you on the plane and tell you that over and over again." Georgie stiffened as his arms went around her. "After I explain what you saw at the hotel."

"What did you say?" As much as she tried to fight it, a little burst of joy bubbled in her chest as Liam leaned his cheek against hers.

"I said I love you. And I'm not letting you go anywhere without me. I'll travel the world with you. Wherever you want to go."

Georgie stepped out of his hold and wiped her eyes with the back of her hand. Liam hadn't shaved, and his hair was loose around his collar. She looked at him, really looked at him. Not only had his face lost the gauntness that it had held the first time she'd seen him on the beach, his eyes held an expression that hadn't been there, either. It was the way he was looking at her. All the feelings that clamoured inside Georgie were mirrored in Liam's face.

"The woman I was hugging at the Fairmont was my agent, Sarah. I hadn't seen her since Vanessa's funeral. If you'd waited a minute longer, you would have seen her husband, Mike, come over and thump me on the back while I was hugging her."

He looked down at her and raised his hand to cup her cheek. "Mike and Sarah are my best friends, and they were coming down to the bay today to meet you. I told them I'd fallen in love with a green-eyed woman who bewitched me." A grin crossed his face. "You'll have to tell me where we're going after Hawaii so I can organise for them to meet us."

"How about Machu Picchu?"

Georgie spun around as Sienna's voice came from behind. "I hope you've got that on your tickets. We have a date there for our birthday in a few months."

"Tickets?" She looked at Liam, who pulled a travel wallet out of his shirt pocket.

"Do you know how hard it is to buy a round-the-world ticket with only a couple of hours to get to the airport?" Liam's grin got wider and he pulled her back to him. "And organise Thelma and Mitzi to look after the house for a few months?'

Georgie's heart started beating again. The ice was melting and warmth filled her veins as she looked around. Sienna and Jack both had smiles on their faces, and Liam was still looking down at her intently.

Oh my God. Georgie hugged the feeling to her before she spoke. Liam loved her? Liam was going to come on her trip with her. And the whole trip? Not just Hawaii? With *her*? Unlovable

Georgie?

This man who was holding her like he'd never let her go? This man *loved* her. Happiness flooded through Georgie and she put her hands on either side of Liam's unshaven cheeks.

"I jumped to conclusions, didn't I?" Georgie let the love flow through her.

"You need to—"

"*Ssh*. My turn." Georgie trailed her hand across the stubble on Liam's chin and put one finger against his lips. "I haven't told you that I love you yet. That's pretty important for you to know, if you're coming with me."

The last thing Georgie saw before she closed her eyes for Liam to kiss her was Sienna wiping her eyes. "Now we've made Sienna cry. And she never cries."

Epilogue

The mist hung low over the lush green mountains and a gentle rain had brushed their faces as the small group walked barefoot on the damp grass. Soft music surrounded them and the guests smiled as the bridal party appeared over the hill. Thelma and Mitzi dabbed at their eyes with lace handkerchiefs, but their emotion soon turned to gentle laughter as Faith dropped her mother's hand and sat on the wet grass and began to tip out the rose petals in the basket she'd been carrying.

"Faith, come on. You can play later." Ana smiled apologetically at Georgie as she picked her little daughter up from the grass and settled her on her hip. "Sorry, the joys of two-year-old flower girls."

Georgie leaned down and kissed the soft cheek of the little girl as Sienna waited for them to catch up. "She's fine; nothing is going to spoil this day."

Sienna smiled at her cousin. "And you've done it, sis. Your childhood dream. First married out of the three of us…and before your thirtieth birthday. One day to go…you just made it," she said drily.

Georgie stood beside Sienna as Ana followed them with Faith. "Only just, sis. It doesn't seem like almost a year since our last birthday, does it? And Ana's next." Ana and Blake had set the date for their own wedding.

The gathering was small. The guests sat in two rows of silk-covered chairs on a grassed terrace, where petals were strewn on the ground in heart shapes. The area was protected from the breeze by a polished dry stone wall. Joe and Magda sat behind Thelma and Mitzi; Sarah and Mike were beside Uncle Renzo and Aunt Lucia.

"Well, you two got to Machu Picchu like you planned, but I bet you never thought it would be for your wedding," Ana said.

Georgie smiled at her two best friends and her heart filled. Everyone she loved was here to see her take her wedding vows with Liam. She looked ahead, past the chairs to where he stood waiting with Jack, Blake, and the celebrant, in front of a small altar. A magnificent vista of mist-covered mountains formed a dramatic backdrop behind Liam, who stood tall and proud. He held her eyes with his, his white silk shirt billowing in the gentle breeze over his loose white trousers.

The music swelled and Georgie stepped ahead. The others could catch up; Liam was waiting for her. She smiled as he took her hand and spoke softly.

"Hello, my beautiful Georgie."

\#\#\#

Later that night in the hotel at the base of the mountain, Georgie rested her head on Liam's shoulder. She closed her eyes and let out a soft sigh as his lips brushed her cheek softly and they moved slowly together on the dance floor.

"You didn't tell me all the news, Mrs. Wyndham," he said softly.

"What news?" She opened her eyes and looked up at this man she loved with all of her heart.

"Look." He nodded in the direction of Sienna and Jack. Jack's hand was resting on the almost-unnoticeable bump on Sienna's tummy, and Georgie smiled.

"She didn't want to take away from our day. She's telling everyone tomorrow."

"I think it's too late." Liam smiled as Thelma and Mitzi threw their arms around Sienna. "They don't miss a trick, do they?"

"I adore them. It was so good that they all came to our wedding." Georgie had missed her family and friends as she'd toured the world with Liam, but the six months they had travelled together had been an experience she would always cherish.

"I've got the tickets for our honeymoon destination in our room." His sexy smile spread across his face, and the inevitable warmth turned Georgie's bones deliciously loose.

"Maybe you should take me to the suite and show me?" Georgie lifted her hands to his cheeks and rested her lips against her husband's. "Where are we going?"

"There's a house on the hill at Hideaway Bay waiting for us." He grinned down at her. "And there are some bookshelves to be finished. Don't know where we can find a good tradesperson, do you?"

Other Books

Whitsunday Dawn
Undara
Osprey Reef (November 2021)

Porter Sisters Series

Kakadu Sunset

Daintree

Diamond Sky

Hidden Valley (2021)

Pentecost Island Series

Pippa

Eliza

Nell

Tamsin

Evie

Cherry

Odessa

Sienna

Tess

Isla

Sunshine Coast Series

Waiting for Ana

The Trouble with Jack

Healing His Heart

Bondi Beach Love Series

Beach House

Beach Music

Beach Walk

Beach Dreams

The House on the Hill

Second Chance Bay Series

Her Outback Playboy

Her Outback Protector

Her Outback Haven

Her Outback Paradise

Love Across Time Series

Come Back to Me

Follow Me

Finding Home

The Threads that Bind

Others

The Trouble with Paradise

Deadly Secrets

Adventures in Time

Silver Valley Witch

The Emerald Necklace

Worth the Wait

Ten Days in Paradise

About the Author

Finalist for the NZ KORU award 2018 and 2020.

Winner ...Best Established Author of the Year 2017 AUSROM

Long listed for the Sisters in Crime Davitt Awards 2016, 2017, 2018, 2019

Finalist in Book of the Year, Long Romance, RWA Ruby awards 2016

Winner ...Best Established Author of the Year 2015 AUSROM

Winner ...Author of the Year 2014 AUSROM

Best Established Author, Ausrom Readers' Choice 2017

Book of the Year (Whitsunday Dawn) Ausrom Readers' Choice Awards 2018

Annie lives in Australia, on the beautiful north coast of New South Wales. She sits in her writing chair and looks out over the tranquil Pacific

Ocean. She has fulfilled her lifelong dream of becoming an author and is producing books at a prolific rate.

She writes contemporary romance and loves telling the stories that always have a happily Ever after. She lives with her very own hero of many years and they share their home with Toby, the naughtiest dog in the universe, and Barney, the rag doll kitten, who hides when the grandchildren come to visit.

Stay up to date with her latest releases at her website: http://www.annieseaton.net

Awards

Book of the Year (Whitsunday Dawn) - Ausrom Readers' Choice Awards 2018.

Finalist (Whitsunday Dawn) – ARRA romantic suspense.

Finalist - NZ KORU award 2018 and 2020.

Winner - Best Established Author of the Year 2017 AUSROM.

Longlisted - Sisters in Crime Davitt Awards 2016, 2017, 2018, 2019.

Finalist (Kakadu Sunset) - Book of the Year, Long Romance, RWA Ruby awards 2016.

Winner - Best Established Author of the Year 2015 AUSROM.

Winner - Author of the Year 2014 AUSROM.